Books by Eleanor Cameron

The Mushroom Planet Books

THE WONDERFUL FLIGHT TO THE MUSHROOM PLANET

STOWAWAY TO THE MUSHROOM PLANET

MR. BASS'S PLANETOID

A MYSTERY FOR MR. BASS

TIME AND MR. BASS

Other Books for Children

THE TERRIBLE CHURNADRYNE

THE MYSTERIOUS CHRISTMAS SHELL

THE BEAST WITH THE MAGICAL HORN

A SPELL IS CAST

A ROOM MADE OF WINDOWS

Novel

THE UNHEARD MUSIC

Essays

THE GREEN AND BURNING TREE

On the Writing and Enjoyment of Children's Books

A Room Made of Windows

a room made of windows

by Eleanor Cameron

Illustrations by Trina Schart Hyman

An Atlantic Monthly Press Book

Little, Brown and Company — Boston — Toronto

LIBRARY OF CONGRESS CATALOG CARD NO. 77-140479
Sixth Printing

ATLANTIC-LITTLE, BROWN BOOKS
ARE PUBLISHED BY
LITTLE, BROWN AND COMPANY
IN ASSOCIATION WITH
THE ATLANTIC MONTHLY PRESS

BP
Published simultaneously in Canada
by Little, Brown & Company (Canada) Limited

PRINTED IN THE UNITED STATES OF AMERICA

This one is for Sylvia and Elston
and is dedicated to the memory of my mother,
January 28, 1889 – September 4, 1970

A Room Made of Windows

Chapter One

She stayed long enough at the front door to listen to their footfalls die along the graveled drive, as if she wanted to taste to the last morsel her furious disappointment and humiliation. Then she flew into the hall past Greg's room, where he was typing as if he had only five more minutes to live, up the stairs, shoved open the door of her own room and slammed it hard enough, you would have thought, to shatter every last one of its ten panes. But they did not shatter. And the cats, who had been sleeping peacefully in each other's arms on her camp cot, leaped in stricken darts of gray and orange through the door beyond and vanished into the blackness under her mother's bed.

"I'm *ashamed* of you —" She could hear even now the breathless voice at her ear, trying to maintain some sem-

blance of privacy and dignity in front of Uncle Phil. "I'm
so *ashamed* —"

"But you haven't any right — you've never gone without me before. My first play — and I've been telling
Addie all week! You promised! Uncle Phil promised!
What will I tell Addie? *Why* can't I go?" She'd broken
free from her mother's grasp and flung it away.

"Because we're going out with friends after the play,
Julia, that's why. And it isn't for a child. We did not
promise you. No promise was made. If there had been,
you would be going." Mrs. Redfern's face had seemed a
stranger's in the lamplight, unfamiliar, inimical. Her eyes
had shone, too close, so as to seem abnormally large, spar-
kling with embarrassment and anger, and Uncle Phil —
but he no longer had a name, becoming in an instant That
One — stood staring down at her unhappily. But no, no,
she corrected herself: meanly, slyly, triumphantly. And
he'd looked round, fumbling with the doorknob, then suddenly flashed her a glance as if he were thinking, "She's
not mine, so I can't say anything — but if she *were* —!"

As her mother and That One walked, invisible, across
the dark grass all blown with the long sickle leaves of the
eucalyptus, "You have my utmost despision," she'd yelled
after them from the front door, "and I'll never forgive
you — never — never — never —" the last "never" ending in a sob of rage, which was the blackest defeat of all.

Now, upstairs, she snatched open the door onto the
balcony and it seemed to sway like a ship in her fury so
that she had to hang onto the railing, and she shouted into

the wind, "Despise — despise —" in a tossed and shaken voice.

But they couldn't have heard. She stood listening with caught breath to the vast, free roaring of the eucalyptus whose enormous trunk shone pale across the garden, and saw a single light trembling through its harried branches high up at the top of the house next door. Mrs. Rhiannon Moore was working in her music room, sounding chords that came now soft and clear, now muffled, now loud, then soft again. Black Bart, the old beaten-up robber cat, yowled once, "R-r-r-r-o-o-o-ow-w!," hoarse and dismal and desolate. The windmill behind Mrs. Moore's house creaked and creaked in its aged timbers, and its dark bulk seemed to lean a little. The wind rested itself for a moment and Julia heard That One's car start up — and go along to the corner — and turn — and that was all.

When she went in again, there was Greg, tall, thin, solemn Greg, too tall for fourteen, with his big tortoise-shell-rimmed glasses shining like owl's eyes and crooked as usual because his intensity made him struggle and sweat as he typed in his closed-up room so that his glasses were always slipping. He looked at her, just looked, then quick, up came a finger and flicked them straight with that habitual gesture of his.

"You're a selfish kid," he said. "Why couldn't you just let her go and have some fun?" He glared at her, then turned and went downstairs again, and Julia threw herself, spread-eagled, across her bed with her hands pressed over

5

her ears to keep out any more words. But before he could get to the bottom —

"*Greg?*"

Silence. Then, from the depths of his disgust, "What."

"Greg, there *is* a word 'despision' —"

"Nope. There isn't."

"But there *is*. There's *got* to be —"

"Well, there isn't. Hey, that's funny." Silence again, while he thought. "There's 'sardonic' and 'sarcastic' and 'ironic,' but no 'sardony' like 'irony,' and no 'sardonasm' like 'sarcasm.' But I think there's 'sardonicism.' " He nosed his way around among these various words, apparently, then crossed to his room, closed the door, and presently the torrent of typing started up again.

Julia put her hands over her scarlet face and whispered, "There is — there *is* —" and sat up and reached onto her desk, which stood by her bed, for the sad old coming-apart dictionary she'd been given when Greg presented his mother with a fine, leather-bound, thumb-indexed one for her birthday. ("Gee, what a present!" Addie had said, staring at it. "A *dic*-tionary! Who'd want that for a birthday present!" "I do," said Mrs. Redfern, "especially from Greg.")

It was awful always to have to use words you weren't sure about, to have to use them in front of people and not just in your own head, and see everybody tickled inside themselves. Felony Franklinburg she'd named her doll, years and years ago when her father was alive, the most beautiful name she could think of and wished it might

6

have been her own. But when she told it to a roomful of her mother's and father's friends, their mouths opened in round black pockets of laughter. And when she asked Greg to show her how to look up words, it turned out "felony" *did* mean a crime, a grave and serious crime, just as he'd said. And over at Aunt Alex's and Uncle Hugh's in San Francisco at Thanksgiving, she'd remarked in front of their company, joining in the grown-up conversation, "Well, admittedly speaking, Berkeley *does* have less fog." And in the merriment that followed, she'd heard some loathly woman chuckle, " 'Admittedly speaking'! Isn't that the cutest thing you ever heard!" And right after this at the table, she'd gone and said "mizzled" for "misled" (she still thought "mizzled" sounded much more mixed up than "mis-led") and Aunt Alex observed to one and all, "Oh, our Julia's quite the word girl!" in that bright, perky tone of hers. These were the moments you did not ever forget, but what Julia could not seem to learn was that there was always another waiting around the corner.

"Despise," but no "despision." She shut up the dictionary, turned out the lamp on her desk, and lay looking up through the skylight at the stars. "You have my utmost despision —" and That One had probably heard and laughed to himself in the darkness all the way along the drive, or snickered out loud, and her mother had probably said, "Phil, don't — the poor child —"

No "despision." So then you have my utmost cold, heavy, unending, undying *despisement.* And she banged her fists on the wall at the side of her bed and knew how everything would be in the future. That One wasn't even her real uncle, just a friend of the family's and manager of the music store where her mother worked, and she and Greg called him uncle only because he'd known them all since before Julia was born. When she stopped banging she heard steps, light and quick, coming up the stairs, and the knob of the door turn.

"Dearie." It was Mrs. de Rizzio, the landlady, who lived with her husband, Frank, and her father, old Daddy Chandler, in the much larger front part of the house. In the darkness, though Julia would not look, she knew that Mrs. de Rizzio, hardly taller than herself, was standing at the foot of her bed. "Julia, what is it — what is the matter?" No answer. Nothing but the sound of Greg's typing and the wind making a hollow, streaming moan across the peak of the roof. "You know your mother doesn't go out very often and how much she always enjoys herself with Uncle Phil. Why must you act like this?" Still no answer, because none would have been possible. "Would you like to get into your pajamas and robe and come in with Frank and me?"

Julia swallowed and forced herself to speak.

"No, thanks, Mrs. de Rizzio," she said with dignity. "I think I'll go to bed."

"All right, then." Mrs. de Rizzio started down, then stopped. "I don't want you to bang your door again like that, Julia. If the panes should break, someone is going to have to pay to put them back, and I wouldn't want your mother to. Now, you remember." The firm, precise words could not have been forgotten, and would not be. The high heels clippeted on down the stairs and Greg's typing never stopped once.

Someone is going to have to pay.

"Cats?" called Julia. "Sandy? Gretchy?" But no lithe, light-footed shapes leaped onto the bed; no cold noses and warm silken sides pressed along her arms. They had crept away, terrified no doubt by the banging, slipped downstairs and out the cat door that used to be Zabero's and that swung on hinges at the bottom of the big door on the back porch. They must even now be hunting under the wind, wild with that elemental joy the wind always sent along their nerves and veins. They wouldn't be in again all night long — not on a night like this!

Boy, what original names, Greg had said, and I thought you were supposed to be so good at names. But those just *were* their names: light, wraithlike, feminine Gretchen and large, hard, daring, orange Sandy. They might have called Sandy Zabero the Second, and Julia had tried when he first arrived, but he wasn't a bit like Zabero, the cat who had lived here when the Redferns came and who had belonged to Mr. de Rizzio. He'd been a huge marmalade cat, spoiled, perverse, even spiteful at times, hiding in the bushes and then leaping out, scratching and biting for no reason except that he was in a mean mood. But Sandy, for all his hardness and daring, was as loving as Gretchy. He'd fight old Black Bart any time, and had. But he'd never put out a claw to his own humans. He and Gretchy

9

would sleep on Julia's bed in the sun pouring through the skylight, their arms around one another in a kind of cat bliss, and she would find them there when she came home from school.

Every day when she got home, she would first of all greet her cats and then give her special knock on the wall. Daddy Chandler in his attic on the other side, where he was working away on his book, would knock back. And Rhiannon Moore would usually be playing something softly or magnificently on the other side of the driveway.

/ At the thought of Daddy writing, she sat up, turned on her desk lamp again, and pulled from her dress front a string necklace, white when new but quite gray by now. On it was her skate key, the front door key, and the most precious key she possessed, the one that unlocked the drawers of her desk. There were two deep ones on each side and a wide, flat, central one, the locks of which Mr. de Rizzio had installed for her as a birthday present. From the central drawer she drew out her *Book of Strangenesses* and turned to the front to her lists of most beautiful and most detested words. Under the beautiful words, which began with "Mediterranean" and "quiver" and "undulating" and "lapis lazuli" and "empyrean," she added "mellifluous," which she copied from a piece of paper Mrs. Gray had given her at school. Then she moved to the page opposite. The place where she acutely suffered all fear and rage and anxiety *wasn't* her stomach, Greg had told her this afternoon when she'd explained to him exactly where she felt these emotions. Because her stomach was right under her ribs, and it was her intestines she must mean, twenty-eight feet of them, he said, all wrinkled and wadded up into that small space she was patting. So now Julia added "intestines" to her list of most detested words: "rutabaga," "larva," "mucus," and "okra." Greg said she was mixed up, and that it wasn't the words themselves she couldn't stand, it was what they meant. She didn't agree, because it was the *sound* of them she couldn't abide.

After her word lists came the lists of "Dogs Alive and Dogs Dead" and "Cats Alive and Cats Dead," which gave the names of all the dogs and cats she'd ever known and knew now. Julia kept these lists in her *Book of Strangenesses* because of what had happened to certain of the dogs and cats.

The claws of Jennie, Uncle Hugh's loved collie, had been heard clicking on the linoleum of the kitchen floor a week after Jennie died and the sound had been so natural, so expected, that Uncle Hugh never hesitated an instant, but just got up and went out to give Jennie her dinner. Of course she wasn't there and never would be. Or had she been? Uncle Hugh said he felt very strongly that she was: there had been no doubt in his mind.

Patchy, a black and white cat of the Redferns', suddenly commenced a habit after the children's father was killed in the war of meeting Mrs. Redfern every day at the car stop where she got off the streetcar a long way from home. It was something he had never done before. Slowly he paced beside her across the wide and windy fields while she wept because of grief and tiredness and despair out there where no one could see her or ask questions. And when she nearly died during the influenza epidemic, he did not leave the foot of her bed, and would have starved if he hadn't been fed in the bedroom and allowed to jump back up again. It was a wonder, Grandmother said, that the cat himself had lived, he ate so little.

Further along, under the last entry, she wrote as she always did, the word *Strangeness,* and then, "I heard somebody talking to a woman down the street today and she called her Mrs. Mendenheal and it seems her husband — Mrs. Mendenheal's — is a doctor. If *that* isn't the strangest thing!"

Now Julia had to stop to think because the moment had come for which she had opened the book, and it was not another strangeness she had to tell, yet what she wanted to say must be put down. And it deserved a new paragraph with a good wide space between the lines about Mrs. Mendenheal and what was to follow.

"I have to write here that the person I used to call Uncle Phil has a new name — That One. He told me a lie and he broke his promise. He said" — but here she had to stop again to get the words just right — "I mean *he made me think he was saying* that he *would* take me to the play. And I told Addie because she's never been to a real play and neither have I — just old school plays, and I've been looking forward to it for days and days. And now Addie'll think I was making it all up and showing off, the way she always thinks and everybody else. He fooled me, and so I will never speak to That One again or look at him or notice him in any way. And that's how it is going to be from now on forevermore." Once more she stopped to think because something further was necessary. "Why did they want to leave me out? They never have before — or Greg, if he wanted to go. But it wasn't Mother's fault because That One is paying and so he was the one who did it. When I came downstairs he was laughing about something and he stopped when I came in, and when he helped Mother on with her coat he left his arm around her. And I hate him." Again she paused, then drew three heavy, denting lines under the word "hate."

Chapter Two

She opened the drawer and was about to put her book away when, instead, unexpectedly to herself, she reached in and drew out some papers from the back. "My story —!" She laid it on the desk and began to read with an ecstatic, soothed sense of surprise — yes! yes! — and felt the same excitement as when she had begun it. It left off halfway through and now she took up a pencil and sat staring at the black window in front of her.

Outside, glimmering like mist in the light from her lamp, the white-painted roof sloped sideways into a valley. Across this valley, on her right, framed in his window, Daddy Chandler's head was to be seen under a light that hung from his attic ceiling. He was working at a large sheet of cream wrapping paper (he never used anything else) on which he was writing in an angular, almost un-readable hand about Lola Montez, the dancer, and her friend, his own mother, who had been an actress in the 1850's in San Francisco. Through the boughs of the eucályptus Mrs. Moore's light still shook among the moving leaves. At this moment she stopped playing and then the whole neighborhood was quiet except for the wind, for Greg was no longer typing. Julia looked down at the last lines of her story, changed a word here and there, then finished the page and went on to another.

It was a puzzling story, like nothing she had ever tried before and the first part of it had been a dream: of finding herself in a theatre hung with tapestries, each of which was the portrait of some person, and the one she most noticed was that of a man with the saddest eyes she had ever seen. Presently the stage of the theatre became a confusion of shadowy shapes and a chorus of voices could be heard, at first murmurous and indistinct, then louder and louder, rising in a mournful chant that seemed to surround her and to catch her up into the midst of those shadowy shapes so that she was taken into their struggle and confusion and carried with them away from the theatre along dark streets that turned and turned, one upon another. She was part of a group who had some plan they were carrying out and though she did not know what the plan was, gradually she began to be filled with shame and terror and dread but hadn't the courage to leave them for she knew that she could never find her way back to the theatre. After a while they came to a certain house where they all stopped, and though no one knocked, the door opened as if they had been expected. And there stood a figure in a mask, and when he took the mask away, she saw the face of the man in the tapestry.

His sad eyes studied her. He stood there in silence looking at her — at her and at no one else — saying nothing, and he seemed to understand why they had come. She felt then that she knew him, and not because of the tapestry, but because they were connected in some way (but how? were they related?) and this filled her with horror that she had come with the others to find him. Before anyone could speak — and here the story stopped, but after all these weeks she still felt the blurred whole of it in her mind and, even though she must go carefully, she was fairly certain of how it must end.

Now she and Daddy Chandler were companions, each enclosed in his own world of striving, yet nevertheless companions. Lost to her surroundings as she had seen Daddy lost to his, she went on writing.

"Perhaps this little room could be Julia's." Those were the words Mrs. de Rizzio had spoken almost a year ago when she first took Julia and her mother around the apartment which Mr. de Rizzio himself, according to his own peculiar whims, had added onto the brown-shingled bungalow with the white roof. The little room was hardly more than nine feet by seven, nothing but a large passageway between the stairway door and the bedroom beyond, but with windows on two sides, a skylight over which a bamboo blind could be pulled in the slanting ceiling, a glassed-in light well with opaque glass in the roof that let in a soft, pervasive glow when the sun was overhead, and a glass-paneled door leading onto a small balcony above the back garden. It was meant to be a sewing room or a sun-room, Mrs. de Rizzio explained; they hadn't thought to take children. Julia, upon entering, knew it at once for her own and saw her camp cot in the corner under the skylight with her desk beside it, in front of the windows opposite Mrs. Moore's back garden. Just beyond her bed would be the big door that opened into a closet, the floor of it hip-high, that extended away into blackness under the roof behind Daddy Chandler's room. And facing the foot of her bed would be the glass-paned door leading downstairs. Her desk would, of course, have a chair, but there would be space for no other furniture. There were built-in shelves, not very wide, by the balcony door, and her books, she thought, would just fill the four of them.

"I hadn't planned on paying quite —" her mother murmured, and you could see her trying to figure the basic necessities in her head, but slowly, because she was not at all good at figures. Yet, Julia knew, what with the windows and the garden and the trees (there was a huge old grandfather oak outside the window at the end of the living room) and someone in the front to be there when neither Greg nor her mother was at home, that Mrs. Redfern was slipping. If Julia did not say anything, but just looked at her mother quietly and strongly, as if there were a cord between them and she was pulling — pulling —

she had a feeling that this room, which would always be hers no matter what happened, would be hers in reality. "How you spoil that child!" Grandmother was always exclaiming in indignation. She never said that about Greg, who came and went in a self-composed world of his own, accepting his surroundings almost without comment. Had he much minded sleeping on the lean couch in Grandmother's living room with his private treasures packed away after his father was gone and their house sold? He never said, only once dryly calling the couch his "bed of Procrustes" because he was too long for it.

When they moved, as soon as she got her camp cot up the stairs, Julia unfolded it, slipped the wooden bars in along the folded-over, sewn sides of the canvas, and pushed it directly under the skylight. Now she could watch the lightning, in case there should be any, and clouds bowling along in stormy seasons, the tops of trees bending and birds being swept about in the air. Sometimes, maybe (and they had later done exactly this), they would come down and light on the glass with their claws tapping, and look in at her, first with one eye and then with the other. At night the moon would shine on her as if she were out camping, and she could watch the cold, patterned stars in warm comfort. As she stood there in her room on moving day, having just folded two blankets for softness and put on the sheets, she held still for a moment and knew something she did not often, in her headlong flight through the days, stop to know: that she was happy and that her happiness was almost too big to hold. *We are here — we are here — we are here!*

Yes, she was happy, and then forgot she was, because she was busy filling up the shelves with her books, arranging them in exactly a certain order she had thought out when she woke that morning.

"We can't get it up, Julia," shouted Uncle Phil, and he meant her desk, she understood at once. He was at that time not even remotely beginning to be That One. In fact she would have said, had the matter been put to her, that she — what? Liked him very, very much, maybe even loved him next after Mrs. Gray, her teacher, who always called Julia's writings her "lit'ry effulgencies," which meant her literary outpourings.

And her literary outpourings *meant* her desk. Julia went pounding down.

"When Zoë and I planned the apartment," said Frank de Rizzio, "we never thought about a girl with a hot red face and greeny-brown eyes and a crop of wild hair wanting an enormous object like this hoisted up the stairs." He stood at the bottom of the narrow flight grinning up at her, holding one end of the desk, and Uncle Phil, partly in the living room and partly in the hall, holding the other, with Mrs. de Rizzio hovering at the banister.

"*Zoë!*" said Greg. He was coming in through the bathroom from the back porch, his arms strained around a large, apparently very heavy box marked in big black letters EGYPTIANS — PRIVATE. "That's a name I never heard.

19

I'll bet this is the only family in captivity with four *z*'s, counting Zabero."

"But my desk!" cried Julia. "Can't you honestly —?"

"Frank's teasing," declared Mrs. de Rizzio. "And you must get it up, Frank. Julia's father made that desk, and she has to have somewhere to work."

So they did get it up, though nobody understood how, because it was broad as well as long, and the legs kept insisting on not being tricked through and around the doorway which was, perhaps naturally, as narrow as the stairs. And when it was settled, there was not a dent or a scratch on its honey-brown surface, smoothly waxed and polished as the last touch to a labor Grandmother had never understood. "What a strange great thing to make for a child Julia's age!" she had said to her daughter. "But that man has never had the least idea of what is fit. It should be for Greg, being the older, and where is it to go in *your* little house? But your husband wouldn't think of a thing like that."

All the same, it wasn't meant for Greg. It was meant for Julia, for she had already, even then, fallen in love with the idea of a desk and had longed for one of her own. And it was because of seeing her father at work at his, and Mrs. Coates in the children's room in the library busy at hers — a desk covered with such highly desirable possessions as paper clips and rubber bands, and a stamp pad and rubber stamps, and a holder for pens and pencils, and various boxes with cards in them, and a big blotter. But then, two years after it was made, it had had to be put into storage along with the Redferns' other furniture. And it had not been out for three.

The story would not do as it was told. It would not slope to an ending, the kind of ending that runs downhill and *feels* finished, as if the people in the story had used up all their emotions, for the time being at any rate. She had written that the man, with the mask in his hand, went back in and closed the door and locked it, that the people she was with broke it open and ran shouting through the dark, echoing house after him. She herself had left them to search wildly this way and that as if for some desperate reason. When she found him at last at the very top, for it was a house of many stories, he turned calmly, as if he had never been frightened at all, and handed her the mask. Then he went down the stairs, and she followed him in bewilderment, and he went outside with the rest of them and stood there as if he were waiting for her. They all turned and looked at her when she appeared at the door and she held out the mask to the man, but he shook his head and spoke for the first time. "Oh, no," he said. "Now it is yours." And she slammed the door and leaned against it, trembling, but could not lock it because her companions had broken the lock.

That was all she could write. She tried again and again to go farther, but everything she wrote after that in an effort to get to the end she had planned, seemed false and added on. This was *her* ending, though whether or not it was the true ending of the story, she could not decide. She

21

read through from the beginning and was astonished. She had never been so pleased with anything she had ever written because, for one thing, it did not sound at all like any other story of hers, and for another, she did not understand it. Why this should be something to be pleased about, she wasn't sure. Even as she read she felt her heart beating hard, hard, as it had in her dream. But beyond the part she knew clearly was dream, the story seemed to her just as compelling. Was it all really hers? And yet whose else, she asked herself, would a person's dream be if not that person's? Don't we ourselves make up our dreams? Surely nobody else does.

She would send off her story now — tonight — to the Saturday page of the *Gazette*. But it was eleven o'clock, the alarm said, sitting not far from her elbow next to the bed. Yet how could it be eleven? It seemed no more than half an hour had passed since Mrs. de Rizzio had gone downstairs and she had turned on the lamp and begun writing in her *Book of Strangenesses*. And why send her story tonight? Because she must, that was all. She must! Besides, she was too excited to sleep.

She listened. Absolute silence between the wind's faint, occasional flurries. Mrs. Moore's light was still on, but when Julia stood up to look, she found that Daddy Chandler had turned his out. He would be in bed now, alone in his attic, making little puffing sounds with his lips the way he did when he took an afternoon nap. She stole downstairs and saw that there was a line of light under Greg's door. She would have to be very quiet. Up she went again, opened her closet door and began digging through the accumulated objects heaped in a tangle near the front. She remembered distinctly having saved for this very purpose a large brown envelope that had come to her mother in the mail, but when she finally found it she discovered that a moldy apple core and a banana skin in the last stages of disintegration were stuck to the front of it. She tossed these aside and labored now to stick a clean piece of white paper over the stains. She then addressed the envelope on the rather smudged square of white and was about to put the pages of her story inside when it occurred to her that it might be well to examine some of the messiest of them. What good to send off what maybe couldn't be read? She went through, "neatening," she called it, erasing crossed-out words and putting in the right ones, and even copying two of the pages. It was now a little past eleven-thirty. Greg's light was off. So were most of the other lights in the neighborhood except for Mrs. Moore's, she discovered when she went outside, having dug up some stamps from the clutter in the buffet drawer where her mother kept them.

She did not remember ever in her life being out alone at this hour. With her mother, yes, a few times, or with Greg, but not alone. The wind was beginning to scurry itself round again and somehow this made being out late more deeply exciting, even a little frightening. She crunched quietly along the drive, holding her story in its envelope up against her chest with her arms crossed over. When she reached the corner a streetcar arrived at the same time and stopped to let someone off. And she saw the pale faces of its scattered riders, drooping and bobbing loosely in undignified public sleep or staring blankly at nothing, all revealed in the streetcar's cold interior lighting as though they were on a stage. They passed on, and she thought, running across the tracks with her head down, poor things, *they* haven't written a story — *they* haven't anything to look forward to. And even as she thought it, there came a raking screech at her heels and a hoarse voice shouting something enraged and meaningless, then a motor revved up and rushed on again down the dark tube of the street.

Prickling with guilt, Julia leaped the curb and kept running. "You never watch — you never think!" her mother would cry. Which was true. And what would she say if she knew Julia was out by herself at almost midnight? And what — what if her mother and That One got home and she wasn't there? She twisted round in her flight along Addie's block to look back, but the street was empty. No car had stopped in front of the brown bungalow with the white roof, and it would take only a second — two or three minutes maybe — to run to the corner, slip her story into the mailbox, and tear back.

Outside Addie's house, wandering along the Kellermans' walk, came a figure, Addie's father, pressing into the wind that gained power suddenly and began sweeping her toward him. And when she was too close to escape, he held out his arms, spraddling himself, knees bent, the way he'd always do to her disgusted annoyance every time she flew down the street on her skates and he happened to be there. She tried dodging him, but he grabbed her with one hand, laughing the way he always laughed, as if this was some big new joke, and then — she could hardly believe it — caught sight of the brown envelope pressed against her chest, and with his free hand, snatched it from her.

Chapter Three

They wrestled on the pavement in the crazily flickering light cast down by the streetlamp through the big elm whose boughs were being wildly tossed in the wind, while Mr. Kellerman kept on laughing and laughing and waving the envelope around over her head. She was breathing hard, puzzled and furious. This was more of his teasing, but in the midst of her struggles she caught a glimpse of the long lantern face with its thin lips, its gaunt jaws, narrow nose and the black smudges wherein his bloodhound eyes sat deep in their sockets, and without warning the horror of her dream flooded her. "Let me have it — you let me have it," she shouted. "It's my story! It's mine — it's mine —" and she doubled up her fists and pounded and pounded straight at him.

26

"What're you out this time o' night for?" he demanded, his words curiously thick and slurred. "You know what time it is? You get on home, now, and I'll —"

But Julia was charging him with a lithe and desperate energy, attacking violently on the side where her envelope was being waved aloft. And then a hand at the end of a long arm was all at once insinuated between them.

"I should like to know, Mr. Kellerman," came a cool, astonished voice, "exactly what you think you are doing? What have you there, and why have you taken it?" Julia and Mr. Kellerman fell apart and Julia looked up and beheld Mrs. Rhiannon Moore, her patrician face filled with disbelief. "*What* is going on?" Without the least effort she plucked the brown envelope from Mr. Kellerman's grasp, his arms fell at his sides, and he regarded her in silence.

"He took it and it's mine," burst out Julia. "It's my story I'm going to mail —"

"What's her ma thinkin' — middla the night!" growled Mr. Kellerman. "She's got no right —"

Mrs. Moore laid her hand on his arm and gave it a pat. "I do agree," she said soothingly. "And I'll see to it that she gets to the mailbox and back in perfect safety. I have something of my own to put in. No need to trouble, Mr. Kellerman."

Again he regarded her in silence, turned his head and stared at Julia, then without comment twisted round and made for his own walk, took his way along it rather wanderingly in that strange gait Julia had noticed when he came out, went up the house steps and disappeared into the black maw of the veranda. Julia had her envelope, battered at the corners and bent right across the middle, once again pressed against her chest and she was smoothing it and smoothing it without even being aware. To Mrs. Moore she wanted to say thanks, but knew quite well she dared not because of a familiar surge beginning to rise full force from a point situated right at the top of what Greg said was her stomach. She ran to the curb, reached there just in time, knelt, and gave up her dinner. When she finished, she straightened and discovered Mrs. Moore at her side holding out a handkerchief. And for the first time she noticed that Mrs. Moore had on a dressing robe over which she'd thrown a coat and that her hair, tied with a cord, hung down her back. She had not very often seen her, only caught glimpses of her through the shrubbery of her garden and had had vaguely the idea of an older woman. What was bewildering was that her hair looked dark in the windy, shaking light, though Julia had thought of it as going gray. Strands of it had come loose and were blowing about her face. How young she looked — how beautiful!

"You know," said Julia, "I think he was drunk."

"He'd probably come out for a little air to clear his head," said Mrs. Moore dryly. Then she was quiet for a moment as they walked toward the corner. "There would be no need, Julia, to say anything to Addie. It might embarrass her. And after all, Mr. Kellerman was right — you shouldn't be out alone at this hour. Isn't anyone at home?"

28

"No," said Julia in an occupied voice, for she was busy going over the fight. "At least only Greg, and he's asleep." Having pictured the whole of her struggle with Mr. Kellerman, it occurred to her now to change the subject. "I'm sorry I was sick. I do that if I get worked up or we're in a car going a long way around curves, or if I eat too much rich stuff. I had two pieces of cake for dinner and I shouldn't have, and then besides that, a lot of other things happened." She waited, because of course Mrs. Moore would now ask, "What other things?"

"I see," said Mrs. Moore. "Well, here we are. In goes yours," and she held open the metal flap of the box while Julia pushed her story over, "and in —" she took a letter from her coat pocket, held it for a second with an air of uncertainty, "goes mine," and quickly she slipped it through as though refusing to tussle with the matter any longer. "A story, I take it," she said as they turned back. "Good luck!" The hand that held Julia's tightened for a moment. "Would you wish me luck too?"

"I'll say I will! Good luck, Mrs. Moore. Is yours a story, like mine?"

"No. There's a story connected with it, as I suppose there is with most letters. But I'm not a writer — I'm a pianist, and a second-rate one at that. Do I disturb you?"

"No, I love it, especially the kind of pieces you play that are sad. I don't know why I like that kind best. They make me imagine things. And then it's nice when I'm writing in my room, and Daddy Chandler's writing in his, and

29

you're practicing your pieces right across from his attic.
We're all doing our special work."

Mrs. Moore looked down at Julia without smiling.
"This is the way you feel? That your writing is your
special work?"

"Oh, yes, the way Daddy Chandler does. He writes every
day without fail, even Saturdays and Sundays. Maybe he
feels he has to hurry because he's eighty-four. The only
time he takes off is to go out to lunch with Mrs. de Rizzio
sometimes, and then to a show, or he takes a nap, or once
in a while he goes for a walk up in the hills with me. He's
the hardest-working old man you ever saw. Is that the way
you feel about your playing, that it's your special work?"

"Yes, I do. Even though I'm not particularly good —
not memorably so — it is without doubt my special work.
I don't think I could live without it."

"But how can you say you're no good!"

"Because I'm not really. Not any more. My son is a concert pianist who travels all over the world, and when he
comes to the house and asks me to play for him, it em-
barrasses me. But of course I always do, for the challenge
of playing for a superb pianist. And just after my first
embarrassment and uncertainty, I sometimes play better
than I have since he was here last."

"Does he live near you?"

"No — in Ireland, where our people come from and
where I was born, in County Cork. He has a very beautiful
home there. But of course he's often away."

"Could I ever hear him?"

"Possibly — the next time he comes to San Francisco. Wouldn't it be fun if we could go over together! But I have no idea what his plans are. Tell me, do you like your story? Are you excited about it — is this why you had to get it right off without a moment's hesitation?"

"Right off!" said Julia. "All the same, I'm bothered. You see, the first part was a dream, and I feel as if the last part, that I made up, is really *more* mine. And then I don't know about the ending. It wouldn't seem to come right."

"You didn't twist it, did you?"

"No, I couldn't. It spoiled everything when I tried, so I left off where it still felt real."

"Good! I should say you have the stuff of a professional writer in you, quite by instinct, apparently. It's far better to write an awkward ending than a false one."

They had crossed the street and passed the entrance to Mrs. Moore's house on the corner, and had come now to the driveway of the bungalow. "Mrs. Moore, would you like to come up and see my room? I'd like it if you would."

Mrs. Moore considered as they walked on along the drive.

"I think not, until your mother's home, what with Greg asleep and everyone else, so it seems."

Julia glanced up at her own windows, wondering how she must look to others, to someone watching as Mrs. Moore might have done, from the outside. And her room seemed to her a globe of light shining softly, with the rounded bulk of the big oak by her mother's bedroom

31

windows at the back of the house looming above the roof line. She could see her lamp, its shade and a little of the stem, and the top of her bookcase by the balcony door, and it was no difficulty at all to imagine the top of her own head and her shoulders bent above the desk.

"You mean my invitation's no good because my mother isn't here? Because I'm a child?"

"No, Julia! But I can't imagine her coming and finding me up there when I don't really know her. If I did, it would be different. And then I'm beginning to have a headache, a rather pounding one — and I want to get home. Sometime I'll —" She broke off and put her hand on Julia's arm. *"Listen!"*

They stood together in the dark garden, their faces lifted. Above the movement of the trees, coming from high overhead, Julia could hear what seemed a multitude of tiny voices, a continuous faraway music made up of bell-like chirrupings that called to one another without cease. On and on they went, as though an endless cloud were passing over, and together with this faint, urgent communing could be sensed — or was it heard? — an indescribable swiftness: the rush of innumerable wings in the distant sky.

"A flock," murmured Mrs. Moore. "An enormous flock of small birds." And even after the last faint voice had gone and the sense of their presence so far overhead had passed, they still stood listening in case another flock should follow. Julia, as they stood close to one another, was aware of herself and Mrs. Moore together in the rich, cool-smelling darkness, held in a hollow of darkness with trees ringing them on three sides and the old mill standing in shadow behind Mrs. Moore's house with its arms becalmed after all these years, rigid, even when the wind blew. They were surrounded by the high irregular shapes of roofs and trees, of sleeping houses with only the eyes of her own room and Mrs. Moore's shining out. From Mrs. de Rizzio's birdhouse came the chirrup of a canary speaking in its sleep and she heard a brushing in the leaves, and then a streetcar went by. "What can they have been?" wondered Mrs. Moore. "What can they have been? 'Little birds like bubbles of glass fly to other Americas' — Western tanagers — yes, flying up from South America only just now because we've had such a late spring. We've had an epiphany, you and I, Julia. Do you know what the word means?"

"No. What does it?"

"Really, it means an illumination, an understanding brought by some brief happening, but for me it's come to mean any sort of rare moment, any treasurable combination of events never to be forgotten. A moment of being." Julia pressed her head against Mrs. Moore's arm but said nothing. "Now you must go in. I'll stay while you unlock the door."

"The night of the birds," Julia wrote. She had pulled her curtains across, undressed, and was about to turn out the lamp, when instead she took the *Book of Strangenesses* from its drawer. "The night of the birds," and tried to find words that would tell just how it had all been, but suddenly she was sick with tiredness and no words would come. "This is the night I've made friends with Mrs. Moore and she mailed a letter she wasn't sure she should mail, at least that's what I think and I mailed my first decent story. And she has a son who plays the piano all over the world and she will take me over to San Francisco to hear him and maybe we will go in back of the stage afterwards so that I can meet him. It's way after midnight. Her light is still on."

Chapter Four

And it was still on at four o'clock. Julia opened her eyes and noticed a faint glow on her wall, and when she got up and looked, there was the light shining through the eucalyptus boughs from the two low, rounded windows, like half-moons, of Mrs. Moore's music room. She turned on her lamp to look at the clock.

"Julia? Are you all right?"

"All right, Mother. Just seeing the time." She'd never even heard them come home, her mother and That One.

"Why aren't you asleep? Do you have to go downstairs?"

"No —"

"Then get back into bed."

And she did, and went to sleep at once.

When she woke in the morning, she lay listening for a moment to the continuous flakes of sound, gradually separating, that fell through the quiet. There was a rustling of paper and little clicking and closing sounds — that was Mrs. de Rizzio working in the aviary. "Cheep, chreep, cheep, churk, chreep, cheep —" and then clear, burbling whistles. Those were the wild birds — the finches and sparrows and blackbirds — and Mrs. de Rizzio's canaries tuning up for the day. Now there was the sound of rushing water and Greg slammed the bathroom door back against the bathtub as he always did, and Mrs. Redfern made muffled clashes in the kitchen directly under Julia's room. Mr. Parcel, who lived on the other side of the de Rizzios, went, "Honk, honk!," blowing his nose good and strong the way he did every morning without fail, sometimes three or four honks instead of two. And Daddy Chandler began creaking his bedsprings before getting up to take his bath, and when he came down to breakfast, he'd be as speckless in a clean white shirt and stiff collar as if he were going to an office in the bank instead of back upstairs to his attic to write.

I love him! thought Julia. I love him best after Mom and Greg, and then who after Daddy Chandler? Why, Uncle Hugh over in San Francisco, of course, even though I don't see him very often any more, but *that* doesn't matter. And then Mr. and Mrs. de Rizzio. But what about Grandmother? Well, she loves Greg, not me. "It's astonishing how that child takes after her father — and not only in looks!" Then came Mrs. Gray, pictured always in

Julia's mind sitting at her desk at school with a sheaf of Julia's lit'ry effulgencies in her hands, her graying brown hair looped up in dips on either side of her face and her spectacles on her nose, her mist-blue eyes very serious and interested behind them. Next, surely, came Addie, and then — the face of Rhiannon Moore, which somehow she could not see other than as a pale oval surrounded by darkness, appeared in her mind. But how can you love someone you've only just met?

She got up and went out onto the balcony to sniff the pungent air as she did now almost every morning of her life (eucalyptus cups were always being crushed underfoot in the drive). In the daylight Mrs. Moore's house and the old mill, which you could scarcely see because of trees, eucalyptus, sycamores, acacias, were revealed as having been painted a soft, barn red, by this time much faded, with white trim. Down below, Mrs. de Rizzio was still busy at the aviary, a little embowered house painted dark green with wire-netting sides and a peaked roof. She was cleaning it out and putting in fresh water and seed and cuttlebone, and she was calling each bird by its own name, which was the name of some great human singer, and talking to them or sometimes whistling in a birdlike rippling way that Julia could never manage. It had something to do with the way you moved your tongue. Soon, having already, at seven in the morning, sent her husband off to his stonemasonry, had her breakfast, and straightened the house, Mrs. de Rizzio would be working among her plants. She was a tiny woman with a head of thick white hair, which she did high in a twisting fold, and she had bright blue eyes and quick-moving ruined little hands like bird claws. She loved brilliant colors and dressed in peacock blues and greens with touches of vermilion, so that Julia always thought she looked like some exotic bird herself moving among her flowers.

"Mrs. de Rizzio!" Julia leaned over the railing above the little woman's head. "Do you know Mrs. Moore? Are you really friends with her?"

Mrs. de Rizzio paused in her work and looked up.

"Why, yes, dearie, I believe you could say I am. We've known each other for a good many years, but she's away a good deal, and then she keeps to herself, practicing on the piano. She used to play in public, you know. Then, too, she suffers from migraine. That's why she looks rather ravaged at times."

"Migraine?" asked Julia. "What's that? What's ravaged?"

Mrs. de Rizzio chuckled as she often did over Julia's questions. "Ravaged means ill or worn-looking, and migraine's an especially fierce kind of headache."

"She said it was beginning to pound —"

"So it does, beyond bearing. I have reason to know. She goes about in her robe some days with her hair tied back."

"That's the way she was last night, when we went —" Julia stopped abruptly, but Mrs. de Rizzio seemed lost in remembering.

"The big house isn't anything like it used to be," she

said, "always so beautifully kept, freshly painted every three or four years, and the lawns front and back so green and smooth and clipped, and the flowers tended and changing with the seasons, and the trees and bushes pruned. That's when Mr. Moore and their son, Oren, lived there — how Mr. Moore loved his garden! He and I always talked about our gardens."

"Did he die, Mrs. de Rizzio?"

"No —"

"Well, what, then?"

But the little woman, as though disinclined to say anything more personal, was already back at her work.

Greg, at the breakfast table, had his atlas propped in front of him, Shepherd's *Historical Atlas,* one of his chiefest treasures, which That One had given him on his tenth birthday and which Greg must know by heart, having fought and refought every kind of battle across its pages, clear back to the times of the ancient Egyptians and Assyrians. He paid no attention to Julia, but kept on eating with his eyes fixed on his book. If allowed, he always read and ate, at least at breakfast, but Mrs. Redfern was adamant about dinner. She was in the kitchen now, singing to herself a silly rhyme out of her English childhood.

> *If a man who "Turnips!" cries,*
> *Cries not when his father dies,*
> *It's a sign that he would rather*
> *Have a turnip than a father —*

"Mother?" Julia had planned to be cool and dignified, but this was going to be difficult because there were certain things she wanted to know and to tell.

"Hello, dear. Uncle Phil went up last night to say good-night to you just in case you might be awake, but I said that of course you wouldn't be and you weren't. He was upset your thinking he'd broken a promise. Of course you couldn't have gone on a school night and I think we were taking it for granted you realized that."

Julia reflected.

"Well, I'm extremely relieved I *wasn't* awake," she said at length. "And all that was, he just had a guilty complex."

"Guilt complex," said Greg, going on staring into his book. And under his breath: "What was the big idea — midnight? I heard you come in."

Julia stopped shaking cornflakes to study him, and up came his strange, almond-shaped eyes, huge behind the lenses of his glasses, and met hers in unaccusing inquiry.

"Greg," she whispered, "I wrote the end of my story and I mailed it. I *did* go out, but with Mrs. Moore. It was all right — and she thinks I'm going to be a real professional —"

"Julia," said Mrs. Redfern, coming in with bacon and with her pot of coffee which she put on the little stained raffia mat Julia had made in the fourth grade, "believe me, you missed nothing by not going. It wasn't a very good play. And you wouldn't have un — I mean, I think it would have bored you." She was rearranging the plates with those quick deft movements of hers that seemed never to waste a motion.

" 'Understood' was what you were going to say. Why didn't you? Maybe I wouldn't have understood, but how could you tell? It wouldn't have mattered and I wouldn't have been bored, even if I didn't understand. Anyway, I finished my story."

"May I read it?"

"You can't, because I —" Her eyes flew up, but Greg appeared not to be listening. "Mother, do you know Mrs. Moore?"

"No, I've tried, but she smiles vaguely over the fence and goes trailing off. I think she's a recluse. I told her once that I admired her playing and that I work in a music store, and she said, 'Records are such a poor substitute, aren't they?' and then looked away into the distance and turned and went in the house."

"What's a recluse?"

"Someone who prefers being alone. Do you, personally, know her?"

"If I ever did, would you care if she came in?"

Mrs. Redfern's eyes, hazel like Greg's, almond-shaped like his and large, rested on Julia.

"Why do you ask?"

"I only wondered. The thing is — I like her."

"But how would you know?"

"I just do," said Julia impatiently.

"I should think," said her mother, "that she wants only

to be left in peace to get on with her music. I have a feeling she's not longing to be friends with anyone."

"Do you know about Mr. Moore? Did Mrs. de Rizzio tell you?"

"Yes. She said that he left one day, just packed up and left, and that she saw him go. She thought that he was leaving on a trip, but he never came back and she hasn't seen him from that day to this. Apparently they're still married, Mrs. de Rizzio said, because Mrs. Moore speaks of him now and then as if they are. But after he left, the house and garden gradually grew more and more shabby, and Mrs. Moore never seemed to care. She tells Mrs. de Rizzio she treasures her solitude, but Mrs. de Rizzio says it's always seemed sad to her when they appeared to be so happy." Holding her cup in her two hands, Mrs. Redfern blew away the steam and now and again took little quick sips. "But I imagine," she said presently, "that when you're elderly and lost in your work, you don't think much about the looks of a place. And then maybe she doesn't have the money for a gardener."

Elderly! Julia looked up in amazement, hearing in her mind the rich, youthful voice with its burred edge, the quality of it fascinating as an actress's, dismissing Mr. Kellerman with quiet authority. She saw the shapely hand reach out and slip the brown envelope from his grasp.

"Are *you* elderly?"

There was an expression on her mother's face that Julia thought might be called amusement.

42

"I'm thirty-five, if you feel that to be elderly, which I'm certain you do. Therefore I should think that to you Mrs. Moore would seem quite old."

Julia was silent, finishing off her cornflakes and then putting a slice of bread in the toaster.

"All the Plantagenet kings of England!" announced Greg suddenly in a tranced voice. He was staring off at some distant procession of pomp and ceremony. "Tarrantarra-a-a!"

No one paid him the slightest attention.

"No," said Julia after a little. "She looks hardly any older than you. And she's not ravaged the way Mrs. de Rizzio said. She's the most beautiful person I've ever seen — well, almost," and her eyes rested consideringly on her mother's face with its level brows and broad forehead from which the glossy hair was brushed back and folded over in a smooth curve from the crown of her head to the nape of her neck. Julia had always admired that curving line and wondered how the thoughtful look her mother's face usually wore, a look enhanced by the smoothly brushed hair, could cover such — *fire*. It was a fire that came suddenly, without warning — leaped up and then vanished to go into hiding again until next time. "Fire and adamant," said Mrs. Gray. "Is that your mother, Julia?" "What's adamant?" "Something as obdurate and imperishable as a diamond." "Oh, yes, that's Mother." And what Julia meant was that the thoughtfulness could never be teased into giving in on a decision. Reasoned, yes, as Greg could reason. But never teased.

43

Mrs. Redfern was smiling to herself and Julia made a design on the tablecloth with her spoon.

"Mother, I don't want you to let *him* come up to my room ever any more. I don't like him. In fact —" and she was going to say with passion, "In fact, I can't *stand* him!" but under that grave, searching gaze, she just could not.

"And who is *him?*"

"You know — *That* One."

A pause. And then: "Greg," said Mrs. Redfern sharply, "I want you to put that atlas away and do not let me catch you reading at the table again."

His head came up. His eyes, slowly focusing, met his mother's. Then the atlas was closed and laid to one side, and the meal was finished in silence.

Greg was already off on his bike. Julia had one, but it lay now in the woodshed, mortally wounded from the day she had whizzed down Vine Street on the other side of Shattuck, lost control, and gone straight into a telephone pole. Why she hadn't been concussed, Mrs. Redfern said she would never know. As it was, Julia had managed to stay out of school for over a week with a bruised face, two black eyes and a sprained knee, the one she had landed on when she was thrown onto the cement. But it wasn't so bad walking to school instead, because Addie didn't have a bike and they could talk.

Julia turned at the back door before going out.

"Where are the cats, Mother? Why aren't they in? They're always in for breakfast."

Yes, when Mrs. Redfern came down in the morning, those two by some sixth sense seemed to know to a split second when she had entered the kitchen and was about to put down their scraps and their bowls of milk. There would be a mad scrabbling on the back steps where both ravenous furry bodies were flinging themselves at Zabero's swing door, wider than either Sandy or Gretchen because he had been such an enormous animal, but distinctly not wide enough to admit both at the same time. Sandy, being the more muscular of the two, always made it in first and at once the two commenced work, each minding its own business, until Sandy might spy the eye of his young friend wandering to his own half-empty dish. At once a threatening growl rumbled in his throat. He would reach out a paw, embrace his dish with a long, protecting arm and coax it away in arcs to a distance he apparently deemed safe, then settle himself solidly between it and Gretchy, presenting her his broad golden beam and tossing suspicious glances over his shoulder every now and then just to make certain he was not being crept up on. And having finished their food, licked their plates, and lapped up every last drop of milk, they would set themselves to burnishing their coats and polishing their ears and whiskers before going upstairs to sleep off breakfast and the long night of adventure with its shocks and pounces and misses, its delectable rifflings of smells, its intoxicating intimations and sweet, brief moments of triumph when the rare capture was made.

"I haven't an idea in the world where the cats are," said

Mrs. Redfern, washing dishes at the sink. And that was all. Julia stood there, but the washing continued in silence. Suddenly she could not bear the silence, the coolness, the sense of her mother's unconcern, of a distance between them which her mother seemed to have no interest in bridging.

"Mother?" No answer. "*Mom!*" And she went and put her arms around her mother's waist and pressed her face against her back. "Mom, I'm sorry about last night." Ah, but she wasn't. That was a lie. Why should she be sorry? What had *she* done? It was just that she couldn't bear, and had never been able to bear, coolness between them, distance, indifference. And at once her mother turned and put her hands on Julia's shoulders and pushed her away so that they could look into each other's faces.

"Don't dislike Uncle Phil. Don't! It makes me terribly unhappy —"

"But why? *Why?*"

"Because he's been kind to us, because he's so fond of us. He's always been, and long before your father died."

"You can't *make* me like him. And don't *say* 'your father' like that," burst out Julia fiercely. "Why do you? It sounds so — I don't know —"

"All right, then, your dad. But I wanted to say that Uncle Phil's building a house up in the hills. You remember when he showed us the plans? And he wants to take us up Sunday to see it, and he thought maybe we could have dinner somewhere afterward."

If there was one thing Julia loved dearly above all else, it was to be taken to dinner, and they went so rarely.

"Would Greg come?"

"Well, of course Greg would come. Why wouldn't he?"

Julia struggled, thinking of all she'd felt, and the passion of her feelings, and of what she'd written: "I will never speak to That One again or notice him in any way . . . from now on, forevermore."

"I don't know," she said at last in a muffled voice, and drew herself from under her mother's hands and went out.

"Gret-cheee? Sa-a-aan-deee?" Gretchy was easier than Sandy to make come a-running, but then Sandy couldn't stand being left behind and he'd never allow Gretchy to arrive first at whatever pleasure was waiting. "Sandy! Gretchy!" But no cats came leaping up and over Mrs. Moore's ivied fence that ran along between her back garden and the de Rizzios', nor was there any sudden rustling in the underbrush behind the aviary, nor beneath the hedge that separated the area where the woodshed stood and Mrs. de Rizzio's clotheslines from the garden itself. Julia turned in a slow circle. Sometimes she never even saw where they came from; they were just suddenly there and she couldn't believe it. And she would try to pick them up both at once and then have to give up on Sandy because he struggled so with all the strength of his lean hardness, and ended up with airy gentle Gretchy who never minded being carried anywhere, her two hind feet resting on the palm of one of Julia's hands and her two front paws arranged neatly side by side on the arm that curved around her. So it always was: Sandy running ahead, tail straight up, and Julia following with Gretch.

No cats. Julia went along the drive toward the street, straining to hear if that was — or wasn't it? — the faintest cry that might be one or the other. She stood still, listening, but the shouts of the children on their way to school drowned what she had scarcely heard, if she had heard it. Out on the sidewalk there was no sign of Addie. But all at once Julia turned and looked up at the windows of Rhiannon Moore's music room. It was as if someone had called her, as she had called the cats, and though no sound had come to her ears, something made her turn and look up.

Nothing was to be seen, however, at those two half-moons, set lower than the other windows, so that their sills, one imagined, would be down near the floor. Julia had always longed to see the inside of that room to discover how it would look, with the light coming in low down like that. Now that it was morning, you couldn't tell if the lamp was still on. But suddenly at one of the windows, slightly raised, near the back of the house, Julia saw a curtain lift. Someone was drawing it aside, it fell, was pulled and twitched, and then lifted again.

"Mrs. Moore," called Julia, and ran back along the drive. "Have you seen my cats?" Now she was looking straight up to where the curtain remained lifted for a moment longer, though no hand or face was visible, and she fully expected the window to go right up and Mrs.

Moore to lean out. But nothing happened, except that the curtain dropped. Maybe Mrs. Moore was not wanting to talk out of an upper window and was even now hastening downstairs and would soon appear at the back door. But she did not. The big squarish old house stood in a lake of utmost silence and sun-flecked shadows under its eucalyptus and sycamores. No shred of sound issued from it, though Julia waited for more than a minute.

Bewildered, she turned away. What have I done? Why aren't we friends any more? But at her own question her face flamed, for wasn't it entirely possible, even though she and Mrs. de Rizzio hadn't spoken loudly, that Mrs. Moore might have heard them talking about her being ravaged and not dressing all day and about her house not looking like it used to? Julia went back along the drive and walked slowly toward the corner, puzzling over the lifted curtain held by no visible hand, that had dropped as if the person inside couldn't have been less interested in Julia and her cats. And yet she rescued me from Mr. Kellerman and was interested in my story, and said I'm going to be a real writer, and we had that epi — whatever it was — in the garden, when the birds flew over.

"What's the matter?" asked a voice. "Why are you pouching?" It was Taddy, the little boy next door who belonged to the Parcels. Taddy's nose, right now, badly needed wiping, but it did not usually. And there had been times when he had crept through the hedge and Julia had told him stories, and he would come over trustingly every now and then to ask Julia or Greg or Mrs. Redfern if he could borrow some candy.

"I'm not pouching," she said. "I'm thinking."

"Does it hurt you, Julia?" he asked, falling into companionable step beside her. "Have you got a stomachache?"

"No, I have not got a stomachache," she said coldly. "Why don't you go away and play?"

"But I haven't got somebody to play *with*."

"Well, go and call him then."

Julia met briefly his studying, puzzled eyes.

"But I told you I haven't got — *who* shall I call?"

"Whoever he is — somebody. You said you haven't got somebody to play with, so why don't you call him? Maybe he'll come."

At the corner she stopped and glanced down at him and then quickly away again, feeling the look in his eyes as if it were an echo of something she herself had felt only a few moments before as she stood staring up in bewilderment at Mrs. Moore's window.

"Today," said Taddy, after thinking it over, "I don't like you very much," and he went back along the block to his own steps and climbed up and disappeared.

Now a thin old dog came by and sniffed at Julia, then ran off on the bias, his front legs aiming ahead but his hind legs seeming to have a different idea, and his fur was so rough and ragged it looked as if he were wearing it rather than growing it. Then there was Addie! Quick, what to tell her? Not about the play — but about Mrs.

Moore saying Julia was going to be a real writer, and about being taken to San Francisco to hear Mrs. Moore's son, somebody famous who played the piano all over the world. But, no — she knew now that that would never happen.

"Julia!" yelled Addie. "Julia!" She was flying along in excitement, her yellow-brown hair flopping wildly around her neck, curving under, curving out as if it couldn't decide which way it wanted to go. "Julia, Julia, guess what! Paul's coming — he's really coming this summer, and he's going to stay weeks and weeks. He's the most — the most —"

Julia waited unresponsively while Addie crossed the street.

"Who's Paul?" she asked, indifferent.

"Well, I've told you a million times. He's my cousin in Canada. They've got this big ranch up in Alberta — that's a province, Gram says, just like we've got states — and my aunt and uncle and Paul are coming to stay in about a month, just as soon as school lets out. We got the letter yesterday —"

"Are they rich?"

"Oh, are they *ever* —"

"But if they are," said Julia deliberately, "why are they going to stay with *you?* Where are they going to sleep?"

"*I* don't know," said Addie happily. "But what difference does that make? Somewhere — we can make room. Anyway, the last time Paul was here, a couple of summers

51

ago, just by himself — I mean, that's the kind of a boy he is, he'll go anywhere on the train, and they let him, even though he's only a little older than us — why, we started a house out in back, but then he had to go home, so this time we're going to start all over again and really finish it. And I'll bet Paul wouldn't mind if you came over and helped. I mean, I can't *promise* —"

At the end of a little silence in which Addie seemed rapt away inside herself, staring down at the pavement and giving occasional hops as though a spring had been released inside of her, Julia said, "You never asked me about the play."

"Oh, *that*." Addie flicked back her hair. "Well, OK, then. Go ahead and tell."

"It was the most marvelous," Julia said in a hushed voice, "It was the most marvelous —"

Addie waited, and then, "What was it about?"

So Julia told her of this beautiful woman who was a famous piano player and who lost her husband — he just suddenly packed up and went away. And she didn't see him for years and years, and she missed him and grieved for him and got thinner and thinner, but more and more famous all the time, and more beautiful. And one night she played at a huge concert and the President of the United States came and everybody, and afterwards, when the crowd of people came up with flowers to congratu-late her, there was the President, and right behind him her husband — after all this time. And he said — but suddenly Julia turned and caught Addie's knowing, merry eye and off they went into peals of laughter, and when Addie could catch her breath:

"Why didn't they let you go? Oh, I bet I get it — school night!"

Chapter Five

Julia ran along the drive calling. The cats had not come home yesterday, nor had they appeared this morning. She never called when she got home from school, knowing quite well — though there was never any need to think about it — that they would probably be upstairs asleep on her bed, or on her mother's bed, or Greg's, or somewhere about the house.

But again they were not. And her old brown spread, freshly washed, hastily dragged up over the crumpled blankets and her pillow, bore no imprint of two cat bodies, nor were there any red-gold or gray and white hairs to tell they'd lain there.

"My cats — my cats —" and Julia, with cold hands and a sick, hollow ache in that place in her middle where she knew and felt all sad or disappointing or enraging or terrible things, ran downstairs and, without watching as she crossed streets, went here and there, up one block and down another at random, calling for Gretchy and Sandy, searching at the top of Mrs. Moore's old windmill, going back to see if they had come home in her absence, then running off again. Once in the dimness of her mother's bedroom, where she had been looking in the closet and under the bed, she caught sight of a blurred, tear-streaked face in the mirror and thought, that's me, Julia Redfern, and I'm caught — nothing can help me — no one. What am I to do?

For a little while, Kenny, Addie's brother, joined in, all vigor and enthusiasm, organizing affairs so that he hunted on one side of Grove and Julia on the other. But when no discovery was made he lost interest and met her at the corner, his slight body hunched, his hands dug in his pockets and his face indifferent. "They're gone — somebody's got 'em. They'll never come back now," he said and turned and walked off in that curious spring-heeled way of his.

And at last the sky began turning blue-green with evening, and the streetlights were coming on. Everybody was going in for dinner — all the children going in when their mothers called, and the fathers driving up and parking. Addie had heard Julia calling and had been hunting with her, and now the two of them ran along the drive and into the de Rizzios' to ask if they had seen the cats yet. But they had not. Julia threw herself down in the swing and sobbed,

55

for now everything was dusky and glimmering, with house lights shining through the trees, ánd she realized that she had given up hope and that her cats would not come back. Kenny had been right.

"But they *will* come back, Julia," said Addie. "You'll see — I'm sure they'll come. Cats always do — mostly," she added faintly. Julia could not answer, knowing what Addie knew, and that her words had been given only in comfort. "I've got to go now — Gram'll be setting the table and she'll be wild at me." Presently Addie got up from the swing and Julia knew that she was walking lightly, quickly across the grass and that she had cared about the cats and had really wanted to find them.

Now Julia looked up and her eyes were drawn at once to the two big half-moons of Mrs. Moore's music room, shining out in the swimming dusk through the boughs of the eucalyptus. Just those and no others in the whole dark house, just as they had shone last night and the night before. She got up and went to the fence, pushed past the stiffly moving gate that opened into Mrs. Moore's backyard and ran up the back steps and knocked softly, then more loudly on the door of the screen porch. No one came. No one gave any sign. Now she ran along the path by the fence up toward the front of the house, then around the corner and up the steps onto the wide veranda where silver-green leaves from the eucalyptus lay in drifts, and acorn cups lay scattered under the old rockers and wicker porch furniture whose paint was peeling and whose cushions were faded and cracked. The cushions too were scattered with leaves, as though no one had sat on them for years. Melancholy and deserted the veranda looked in the lonely light from the streetlamp.

There was no answer to her ring when Julia tugged on the bellpull, and presently she tugged again — and listened — but there was nothing, no stir, no faintest step, no creak of board.

Later, after dinner — which Julia scarcely touched — she went in and asked Mrs. de Rizzio if she had seen Mrs. Moore go anywhere or seen her at all, or heard her play.

"No, dearie. I worked outside a good long while, back and front, but never saw her once, nor heard her at the piano. She probably went out the front while I was in the back, and left the music room light on by mistake."

The cats had started to be missing Wednesday morning and it was now Friday. Julia would not go to school.

"But Julia, dear, what good will it do?" asked her mother. "You can't stay home day after day. I will call the pound, and I'll put a notice in the paper. But you must go on with your life. Greg did when he lost Smokey. And Greg was younger than you are now."

Julia looked across the breakfast table at Greg and he was listening but not saying anything. After Smokey had been killed, when Greg was nine, he said that he was never going to love another animal as long as he lived and he never had — liked, but not loved. All the same he must mind about the cats because he had gone out Wednesday night and hunted for them.

"Greg knew that Smokey was gone," said Julia. "He saw it happen, but I don't know anything. I don't know where Gretchy and Sandy are. I don't know who has them, or if anybody has them, or if they're being fed, or if they're hurt. I can't go to school — I wouldn't be able to do anything. Don't make me."

And Mrs. Redfern did not. She telephoned the school and told them what had happened. She put a notice in the *Gazette* to appear the next day, and she phoned Julia at noon to tell her that she must eat, but Julia ate nothing. It was so strange, Mrs. de Rizzio said, that *both* cats should be missing. Who could carry Sandy away? No one could. In the afternoon Daddy Chandler came up to Julia's room and got her and they went out and walked and it was good to press close to him, to feel his warm hand around her own and not say anything but to feel his concern and love for her. As they walked, Julia called, but without hope, and when they got back Daddy asked her if she wanted to come to his attic and stay with him while he wrote, and talk to him whenever she felt like it. But she said no, she felt she would rather stay out in the garden swing and think.

She sat there thinking and listening. Why was it — *why* was it — that every now and then, in the midst of the cars passing and sometimes a streetcar rattling along on Grove, it would seem to her that she heard a cat's cry? Was it only because she wanted so intensely to hear it? And when the cry came and she sharpened her senses to try and catch the next, should there be one, a flickering

rush of leaves in a sudden gust would rise, the men fixing
the telephone cable would shout, and she could not decide
whether it had been all imagining. But why should she
keep imagining? Why the faint, echoing ghosts of cries?
Where, yesterday, had she been most sure, then lost her
sureness and kept running? On the path beside Mrs.
Moore's house on the other side of the fence!

Without the faintest doubt in her mind Julia got up,
went over to the gate, pushed it, went up Mrs. Moore's
back steps and turned the knob on the door of the screen
porch. It was not locked; neither was the door of the
kitchen. When she went in she was aware only that there
were pans on the stove, dishes on the table as if someone
had been eating and had got up and left it all, and there
was a stench of sourness and decay. The door leading into
the dining room stood open, but that other door, that
closed one over there, might lead to the basement.

When she opened it, Sandy and Gretchen came streak-
ing up straight into her arms where she knelt to receive
them.

Julia lay in bliss on the linoleum in her own kitchen,
flat on her stomach with her chin propped on her folded
arms, while Gretchy and Sandy ate for the first time in
three days and two nights. She had divided between them
all the food cats might like that she could find in the ice-
box, and had mixed milk with egg as a special homecom-
ing treat. Now she watched with delight the beauty of
their smiling mouths opening and closing, and noted how

delicately they ate, with what speedy neatness and precision in spite of ravenous hunger. She noticed for the first time since they had come to live with her that the end of Sandy's nose was a triangle of deep orange in contrast to Gretchy's pale pink, and she examined closely the way the fur lay flat and smooth along their noses as if clipped short up into a semicircle at the bridge. She noticed, too, for the first time, that they had a little clump of the finest whiskers, almost invisible, springing up just above the inner corner of each eye, a brief, tall eyebrow. She noticed how the hairs fined out just in front of their ears, how on the inside of their ear tabs the hairs were long and curved, reaching out as if to catch whatever vagrant, valuable vibrations might be floating by that could be of use to a cat. Her hand went out and rested lightly, almost unbelievingly first on one head and then on the other.

Now she rolled over onto her back and stared at the ceiling. How could anyone shut up two animals in a basement and then go off and leave them without food? Why had Mrs. Moore done this? Had she wanted them to starve? Did she secretly detest cats because they caught birds, and she herself loved them and knew their names, and if you went over and looked in her basement would you find bones scattered down in the dark and dozens and dozens of little cat skulls? Julia sat up. Her mother had said that Mrs. Moore was old and Mrs. de Rizzio said she was ravaged, but she was neither old nor ravaged. She was young and beautiful, remembered Julia, at least the other night in the dark with the wind blowing her hair around her face. How could a woman like *that,* the one she had seen and who had taken her hand and walked home with her to be certain she was safe, want to starve cats in her basement? She is a witch, thought Julia, who changes and changes. And why didn't she answer the bell after lifting her curtain?

Julia got up, as sure as she had been the first time, and went out and ran across the garden, pushed open the gate and went up the back steps and into Mrs. Moore's house, and stood in the middle of that horrible-smelling kitchen.

"Mrs. Moore!" she called, and did not stop to wonder if her voice trembled from fright or from fury. "Mrs. Moore," loudly and clearly, "are you at home? I want to tell you — *I have my cats. Why did you shut them up and starve them?"*

She stood still, listening, hearing her own blood throb in her ears and her own heart leaping in her chest. Then something fell to the floor overhead, something heavy and solid that made a reverberant thump. And she thought she heard a voice calling — one word — very faintly, far off, as if not coming from any room in the house at all, but from far away outside. She stole into the dining room and from there into the hall and stood listening at the foot of the stairs curving to the upper floor. She was aware, as she stood, of a tall old clock near the front door, whose slow *tock — tock — tock — tock* increased the potency of the house's silence so that it seemed to grow heavier or to swell toward some unendurable limit. When she could bear the silence no longer, "Mrs. Moore?" she called.

Again the voice was heard briefly, but what words were spoken she could not tell. She advanced hesitantly up the stairs, running her palm along the banister which gleamed in the light that penetrated the fan of many-colored panes above the front door. She stood for a moment in the upper hall, then turned and went toward the back of the house to a room through whose windows she could see trees and a part of the old mill.

When she reached the threshold and looked in, she saw Mrs. Moore lying in a huge dark bed with a high head to it, and had a sense as she stepped forward, though she did not reflect on these impressions now, of green and silver, of long fine lace curtains, of the shadows of leaves moving on the carpet and scattered rainbows glinting on the ceiling from sun striking cut glass on the dressing table, so that with the pale colors and the swimming rainbows, it was as if the room stood under water, waveringly, in green-gold light drifting in through leaves pressed against the windows.

"Julia —" said Mrs. Moore, as though she had been waiting for Julia for a long time.

"Yes, it's me, Mrs. Moore. Are you sick? Have you got migraine?"

"Julia, the cats, I couldn't — yes, I've had migraine." Her voice, with its slight roughness that Julia would always remember, stopped and Julia waited. "The cats came in with me," Mrs. Moore went on. "They wanted to explore — was it after I left you? And I don't — I don't remember letting them out. I thought I heard a door bang when the wind came up again —"

"That was the basement door. Gretchen and Sandy were down there."

"All night and all day has it been? I tried to get up — I think I did —"

"Yes. You pulled the curtain."

"I heard you calling. When was it you called?"

"A lot of times. Wednesday and Thursday and today. But they're all right now. I got them — they're fed. What can I do?"

"No, child, don't come near. It's the migraine does it to me. Don't look." She put her hand up to her face and turned her head away. "Will you get the doctor? His name —" There was a long silence during which Mrs. Moore seemed to be thinking with one hand resting across her eyes, and Julia had time to see that the room, which extended the width of the house, was papered in silver and gold and soft green, that the rug was a silvery green, that the comforter on the bed was a faded mulberry and that the furniture, carved like the bed, stood dark and rich against the pale tones of the room. She saw a heavy cut-glass pitcher lying on its side on the rug at the foot of the bedside table and knew that Mrs. Moore had reached out and pushed it over the edge to tell her to come. Splashes of water lay around it and under its lip. "My doctor's away and I can't think of the other one I've called. Julia —" Mrs. Moore lifted her arm and pointed. "Will you look on my desk, in the little book?" Julia found it by the phone, but the names when she read them out recalled nothing to Mrs. Moore's mind. "I can't think!" she said again in a despairing voice, and Julia put the little book down.

"I know a doctor. He's up the street and I'll go and ask."

"And, child, when you come back, will you make me a cup of tea and some toast? Oh, that would be comforting! I've had nothing since you and I walked in the wind in the middle of the night. Didn't we meet Mr. Kellerman? And then we heard the birds. What did I say they were?"

That evening Julia was trying to clean Sandy. He'd been out again and had come back with a smear of particularly repulsive-smelling oil streaked along his back.

"Sandy," she said, scrubbing away at him with a soapy cloth, "*why* do you get so dirty? Gretchy never does."

"But that's what you get for taking in an explorer-type cat," said Greg, leaning against the kitchen door and drying a dish every now and then. He was deeply content that the cats were back and he seemed to want to be in the kitchen with everyone.

"Sandy's the most curious beast I've ever known — you'd think he was a Siamese," observed Mrs. Redfern. She turned to look down at Sandy and Julia, and Julia felt as she scrubbed how peaceful they all sounded, and how peaceful this kitchen was, and the whole house, after the misery of the past few days. They were together again, the five of them, three humans and two cats, because Gretchy was there too, lying on the linoleum not far from

Mrs. Redfern's feet watching Sandy being cleaned. She never wanted it any different from this, Julia told herself, the five of them together, living in this place with the enormous old oak outside the window where they ate, and Mrs. de Rizzio's garden, and her own room with all its windows and her desk and the skylight and the balcony looking out over everything, and Daddy Chandler next to her in his attic, and Mrs. Moore next door and Addie up the street. Everything was as it should be . . . perfect, perfect.

"Mother, don't call Sandy a beast."

"But I didn't mean it in a pejorative sense."

"What's 'pejorative'?" asked Greg, wiping and wiping away at one dish with a blank look on his face.

"Belittling, depreciating, denigrating."

"You're like Sandy, only with words."

"So'm I," said Julia, getting a better grip on Sandy who was struggling to be let go. "Only I couldn't say 'pejorative' at school. They'd think I was showing off and I guess I would be. But they think that sometimes anyhow, when I'm half having fun and half putting on."

"Use the big words to yourself, then," said her mother. "It's just as good — better, even, because the enjoyment's secret."

"But I never *can* be secret! I always —"

"Oh, let the blamed cat alone!" burst out Greg in his hoarse voice that cracked every now and then, and he sounded as if Sandy's struggles were his own. "Always cleaning something — that's women," he said bitterly.

"Always caring about the most stupid things like the handles on purses and where beans are on sale and how long flowers last in the house and how often they have to dust. All the things that don't matter. I wish my room could be let alone. I wish *I* could be let alone."

"Which reminds me," said Mrs. Redfern tilting up the dishpan and sloshing the water down the sink. "Your ears, Greg. I noticed them at dinner. They're pretty bad."

"That's a gross gronculation and a ferditudinous falsehood. I worked on them not even a week ago."

"Well, work on them again. They're like that gloomy dungeon of yours. How you can *stand* it —"

"But I'm a withdrawn sort of character — it expresses me."

"I don't care what kind of a character you are, and I don't care what it expresses, that room drives me crazy."

"But *why*, Mom? It's not your room. Nobody sees it but me. Now, isn't that the truth? Why must I keep my room the way society thinks it should be kept when nobody sees it and I'm comfortable in it?"

"Society's got nothing to do with it, Greg Redfern. I will not have a pigsty in this apartment, gathering dust and moths and silverfish. Now, you listen to me. You make your bed every morning and put up the blinds and open the windows. Just *do* it."

"But you still haven't come to grips with the central question of why I should do what society dictates when my room is mine — private. You haven't been honest with me, because I don't think you really —"

"Oh, *boys,*" said Julia, and she let Sandy go and he streaked for Zabero's door.

"And let's not hear about boys from you, Julia," said Mrs. Redfern, "not with that closet of yours in the state it is. It actually stinks — no other word — and I think it must be that horrible old untanned rabbit skin of yours you used to have on your desk. I wish to heaven Sandy *had* torn it to ribbons. You might as well start work right now," and she wrung out the dishcloth, wiped her hands, and left to have a word with the de Rizzios.

"Mom's gone off her crumpet again," said Greg gloomily, "just when everything seemed pretty pleasant. I don't know why she gets this way, and always when you least expect it. I mean, you're not *prepared.* And she never makes any sense."

Julia went upstairs and glared into her closet. Then she shut the door and went over to her desk and forgot it.

"A strange and terrible thing," she wrote presently in her *Book of Strangenesses,* "is that because Gretchen and Sandy starved for three days and two nights Mrs. Moore and I are now good friends, *real* friends.

"After I called Dr. Mendenhall (it isn't Mendenheal — Mend-and-heal — the way I thought, which is a *shame*), I went downstairs and put the kettle on and cleaned up the kitchen while the kettle was boiling and I found out what that smell was, only an old meat paper in the wastebasket under the sink. And I was thankful to find this out after the sickening thought about cats I'd had when I came into Mrs. Moore's house hunting for Gretchen and Sandy, and

I was ashamed of having this thought. I threw out the sour cream on the table and the stuff in the wastebasket and opened the windows and after that the kitchen smelled definitely better.

"When I made the toast and took up her tea with it on a tray which I made as neat as I could Mrs. Moore was pleased. And when I went to her with the tray she didn't say anything and I saw she'd gotten out of bed and combed her hair which *is* dark but with gray in it, and she'd put some powder and lipstick on but I could tell she is old. Only it doesn't matter because I like her so much anyway and I still think she is beautiful only she looked pale and I guess ravaged. I told her how I made tea for my mother a couple of months ago when she was sick and left the pot fallen over on its side under the tea cozy and ruined the top of the buffay. And when I went up with her tray I spilled the butter on the rug and the stain is still there and that made her laugh that I'd tried so hard and wrecked everything — Mrs. Moore laughed I mean, not Mom. When Mrs. Moore sat there in bed with her tray and her pillows fluffed and the sheets all neat, she said this is what she'd loved best when she was a child in Ireland, not being sick but getting better and being taken care of, with a fire in the fireplace in her bedroom and meals being brought and being cozy in her own bed with plenty of books to read. I know what she meant because that's the way I always feel, but I've never had a fire in a fireplace in my own bedroom. I wonder what it would be like. The last fireplace we had was in the little house.

"I asked her about the migraine and she said it is as if your head is being squeezed in a vise, that it's a wave of pain that steals over bit by bit and presses tighter and tighter and she held out her hand and closed up the fingers slowly one by one into a fist and said that after a while you can't stand it and then you pass out. She said when she finished the toast and tea that her head didn't hurt any more and she just wanted to lie there peacefully and look at how beautiful everything is. She said she always felt after migraine as if she'd come back from limbo, not hell, but something much worse that has no name. I've had two very bad pains. One was when I came to after I went into the telephone pole and the other was when I thought I'd lost Gretchy and Sandy. I wonder if I'll ever have a pain like Mrs. Moore's. I don't want to but I'm pretty sure I ought to have all kinds of feelings and pains if I'm going to be a writer."

Chapter Six

She woke saying "Saturday!" and saw herself racing to the corner where at four in the afternoon Greg and the other boys would be sitting cross-legged getting their papers ready to throw across lawns and onto porches. Each would be slapping one side of the paper over so as to tuck the folded edge neatly and firmly into the open one, then tossing the paper onto his own pile. A mingling of eagerness and anxiety would sharpen painfully in her stomach as the day slowly passed and that moment drew near when she could actually kneel on the sidewalk with the Young Writers' Page spread flat, while her glance, in not more than twenty seconds, would sweep the whole sea of print, and if it did not at once pounce upon her own name, would dart swiftly from column to column.

At eleven, when the mail arrived, there was, besides two bills, a circular, and a letter for Mrs. Redfern from Great-Aunt Jane Whiteside in Middleboro, Connecticut, one for Miss Julia Redfern from K. Penhallow, 1080 Martins Lane, Berkeley. It was addressed in a peaked, curiously cramped hand, the downstrokes revealing minute jogs and tremors as though the fingers that had penned them were stiff, possibly uncertain, possibly extremely old. Julia stared at the envelope: it was pale gray with almost invisible thin white stripes, the paper thick and the ink rich black. Though she had never taken this trouble in her life, she went thoughtfully into the house and got a little sharp-bladed paring knife. When she reached her own room she shut the door, folded herself up beside the cats and with care slit open the top of the envelope, for she had a feeling, because the name of the sender was sacred, that she would want to keep this letter forever inside the back cover of her *Book of Strangenesses.* She unfolded the sheet and read:

Dear Julia,

Your story "The Mask" interests me enormously, especially when I consider the age of the writer. There is something about it that makes me feel you must be a rather unusual person. I should be very pleased if you would come and see me so that we can talk about it and so that I can meet its author. Will you phone

and tell the housekeeper if you would be able to drop
by around 3:30 or 4 after school on Wednesday next?

Cordially,

(Mrs.) Kathryn Penhallow, Editor
Young Writers' Page

A phone number was given. Julia sat looking away,
stunned, trying to work up a fresh image of Mrs. Penhallow, whom she had always seen in her mind as someone
tall and handsome and decided, wearing a tailored skirt
and crisp blouse, sitting at a large desk and making notes
on the children's manuscripts with a firm hand as she divided the accepted from the rejected with neither hesitation nor regret. Why she had pictured her this way, she
did not know. Was it her name? But now Mrs. Penhallow
had suddenly become gentler, kinder. She worked more
slowly. She had become less brisk. And though the peaked
writing was as elegant, despite the jogs and occasional
tremors, as the paper and the black ink, she had become
older than that handsome dark-haired woman in the crisp
blouse who sat at a commanding desk covered with papers.
Maybe, even, thought Julia, she did now and then hesitate
and regret.

But not about me — not about me! sang inside of her.
She leaned over Gretchen to bury her face in the sweet-
smelling gray and white fur and Gretchy, in her sleep, at
once started up a steady purr. She was lying on her side in

72

a frieze position: her legs stretched out as though she were running and her tail lying above her back in a curve. "What's a frieze position?" Julia had asked her mother when she called it that. "Like a cat on a bas-relief — a flat carving," answered Mrs. Redfern. Yes, Gretchy was, right now, exactly that kind of cat. As for Sandy, he lay on his back with his forepaws drooped over, his hind legs fallen apart and his creamy belly revealed, looking, what with an expression of ineffable content on his sleeping face, vulnerable and endearingly foolish.

She must call and speak to the housekeeper. Above everything, she did not want to, but there was no way out if she was actually to go to the house in Martins Lane and hear Mrs. Penhallow tell her what a very unusual and remarkable young person she was and talk to her about her story. She went downstairs with her letter thinking how she would phone her mother directly after the call to Mrs. Penhallow's and then go in and tell Mrs. de Rizzio and Daddy Chandler of this astonishing happening.

"Yes, Julia," said the quiet voice on the other end of the wire, and it was not the housekeeper's but a man's, a kind voice, neither young nor old. "My wife has told me about your story and about writing you, and that you would call. Good — three-thirty then, on Wednesday. She'll be expecting you and she'll be pleased you can come. Good-bye."

"Good-bye," whispered Julia, or at least in a voice so breathless as to be scarcely above a whisper. She hung up with a cold hand, her heart still leaping foolishly and wildly in her chest. Why is it embarrassing, even frightening sometimes, to call someone you don't know even when the call is about something happy?

The music store line was busy, and still clasping her letter, she ran into the de Rizzios'. But the little black Franklin stove, giving out dying snaps and crackles from its morning fire, was all that spoke in the tidy kitchen. Caruso in his cage in the sunny bow of windows where the breakfast table stood, tossed seeds about, cheeped once, and sharpened his bill vigorously on a bit of cuttlebone. "Mrs. de Rizzio?" The little woman was not in her blue and white bedroom off the kitchen and Julia turned and ran into the back hall and up an open, uncased flight of stairs to Daddy's attic.

She turned the knob slowly, soundlessly, and pushed open the door. Yes, there he sat at his desk, writing away, completely absorbed, and if you listened you could hear his pen in its rapid flight across the surface of the paper. There was no other sound in the attic except a fly buzzing and now and again dashing itself against a windowpane. A beam gave a loud pop somewhere in the roof. Julia stole across the floor on tiptoe and stood behind the old gentleman, watching him trace line upon line, quickly, quickly, as if trying to finish before there should come a tap on his shoulder and a voice in his ear saying, "That will be all for now, Daddy Chandler." She could make out no single word from where she stood of Daddy's angular hand, as though it were written in some foreign language.

And whether it was actually the story of his own life, or a history of the early days in San Francisco, contained in that pile of papers gradually thickening, month by month, on a shelf nearby, no one was certain, not even Mrs. de Rizzio herself.

Now the fly droned off through a ladder of sunlight under the heat-baked rafters, which gave off an aromatic, noonday scent. All at once Julia sneezed. Daddy Chandler stopped writing, appeared to cogitate, then turned and studied her over his spectacles in blank astonishment.

"I declare!" But something in his voice betrayed him.

"Daddy!" shouted Julia. "Daddy Chandler! You knew all the time." She hugged him and planted a kiss on the top of his bald head around which fine, flyaway white hair stood up from being rumpled as he wrote, and thought, and wrote again. "You were just going to go on letting me *stand* there —"

The old man laughed silently until the tears rolled down his cheeks. Then he gave a final gasp and a little cough, and Julia settled herself on his desk while he took from his pocket a fine linen handkerchief, beautifully fresh and white and smelling faintly of cologne. He wiped his eyes and carefully polished the lenses of his spectacles. Then he brought out a couple of big old-fashioned mints, of which he always kept a supply in a paper bag in his pocket, gave her one and popped the other in his mouth. Silently she handed him her letter and watched with grave joy while he read. When he had finished he said, "Mm-*mm!*," folded the letter, returned it to its envelope, then leaned back in his chair and regarded her.

"So it has begun," he said.

"What has begun, Daddy — *what?*" she demanded, knowing perfectly well but wanting him to say.

"Your career."

"But it's been here all the time," and she leaped off the desk, whirled around, and threw herself onto his enormous bed, dark and antique like Mrs. Moore's, with a carved head and foot rolled back along the top in scrolls. She bounced, turned on her back and bicycled vigorously for a moment or two, then looked over at him.

"Of course," he said, smiling at her. "But now the news of it from an editor is signed, sealed and delivered. And one of these days a book will be published with the name Julia Caroline Redfern on the cover. I'll wager it will."

Julia bicycled thoughtfully, then her legs flopped and she lay there, straight out, with her hands crossed on her chest like a medieval queen on a sarcophagus. "But you first, Daddy," she said presently.

"Though I'll not live to see it," he said.

She sat up sharply. "You will — you will!"

"But it all has to be copied, and I haven't the time. There's still too much to put down, and the whole thing ought to be done over again to get it just the way I want it. It's very rough."

"Then *I'll* copy it," cried Julia. "I'll learn to type, because you always have to send off things to real publishers typed. I'll learn, and I'll type out every bit of it for you. I promise you I will," and she went over to him again and sat on his knee and gave him a tight long hug. "I promise." And she felt, as she sat there with her arms around his neck, that she had made a pact, a most solemn and unbreakable pact.

Julia was so elated that when Uncle Phil arrived on Sunday about two in the afternoon to take them up to the new house, she couldn't, somehow, keep distant and cool. When she came down dressed ready to go, he was sitting at the table.

"Julia, are you still angry?"

She only shook her head, then went over to him with her letter. After he had read it, he folded it the way Daddy Chandler had, put it back in its envelope and laid it on the table. He regarded her for a moment and she found herself meeting his eyes shyly. She felt new and stiff and strange with him, as though she hadn't known him very long instead of all of her life.

"It deserves a celebration," he said. "How would you like to have dinner up at the Piedmont Hotel, out on the veranda where we can sit and look out over the whole city and the bay, and the lights will be coming on? Have you ever been up there at night?"

Her eyes widened; she shook her head slowly without speaking.

"We've never been up there at all, let alone to eat," Greg said in a certain quiet tone he had, by which Julia knew exactly how pleased he was. He looked nice for a change, dressed in his good suit, but the sleeves were too short. It was strange how right now he wasn't at all as homely as she usually thought he was.

"And you can have whatever you want — on this special night," continued Uncle Phil. He looked over at Greg, then quickly up at the children's mother, then back at Julia.

"You spoil us, Phil," said Mrs. Redfern, but she sounded lighthearted and as if she was ready to be spoiled in any way Uncle Phil had in mind. "Let's go now. I can't wait to see what's happened to the house since last time."

So she had seen it before then? She'd never said.

They got into the car and on the way up into the hills, Greg teased Julia. Her letter was getting shabby, he said, being shown all over the neighborhood and would be in tatters inside of a week. But she didn't mind everybody laughing. She'd only run over to Addie's with it, she told them, because she and Addie always wanted to know things about each other, and she'd had some books due back at the library so there was no reason not to take the letter along to show Mrs. Coates in the children's room. She was interested in Julia's writing and everything connected with it and always looked at the Young Writers' Page to see if she had a new poem or story. And then when Mr. and Mrs. de Rizzio got back at dinnertime, naturally she went in to show them because they were like her own family. But she hadn't, either, taken it all over the neighborhood. Mrs. Moore wasn't even at home. After two

78

solid days of shaking rugs and the dust mop out the back
door and dustrags out of windows, airing blankets, putting
washing on the back line, sweeping both the veranda and
the front walk, and beating off the cushions of the wicker
furniture, Mrs. Moore's sister had taken her away. She
didn't look a bit like Mrs. Moore — just ordinary — and
the evening before they left she had a talk with Mrs. Redfern over the back fence. Julia was there, too, but as far as
Mrs. Moore's sister was concerned, she might just as well
not have been. Julia was not looked at once.

"My dear," the sister said, "I love Rhiannon, but even
I have to admit that she is no housekeeper. Oh, my — well,
I won't go into *that!* This huge old difficult house is *such*
a mistake, I think, and I fully intend getting her into a
small apartment near me. I mean, at her age, we all have
to be sensible. Now, I'm much younger, but I simply determined I would have, sooner or later, to get rid of most
of my possessions and *consolidate.* That's what a person
has to do, whether he likes the idea or not. He finally has
to face that necessity. But do you think I can get this into
Rhiannon's head? You should hear the discussions. You
know, my dear, you may not realize it, judging from ap-
pearances, but she is a *very* strong-minded woman —" and
on and on and on for about a half an hour.

Julia had known right off that she couldn't abide Rhiannon Moore's sister, and said so now. She and Greg and her
mother and Uncle Phil discussed the subject thoroughly
and all agreed that people have no business pushing
themselves into their relatives' lives and that everyone

79

should be his own boss and make up his own mind about what he wants to do.

She was happy, Julia thought. She was in Uncle Phil's car, going up to see his house, and there they were laughing and joking! She no longer felt that he was That One, and not because of having dinner at the Piedmont. For a moment she felt a stab of guilt, going back on herself as she had done, breaking her promise to herself after all she had written in the *Book of Strangenesses*. Then she forgot and went on laughing and talking with the rest of them.

But how quickly a day, a mood of happiness, can change. It takes only a few seconds, a word or two, a single, unreflecting gesture.

Her mother and Uncle Phil stood at one end of the long bare floor that would be the living room; they were looking over toward the university across a tossed sea of foliage out of which lifted, far off, the white spire of the campanile. Greg, whistling erratically in a plaintive, absentminded way, explored the skeleton shapes of other roofless rooms composed of joists and rafters and uprights. Sunlight laid the shadows of the rafters across them all and across the pinkish-golden floors; a light, flirting wind brought down from mile upon mile of open hill country the vagrant scents of warm sage and dried grasses. Julia stood alone gazing out over Berkeley. On this, the city side of the house, a maze of diminutive streets stretched away down there busy with a twinkling traffic along Shattuck and Grove and Telegraph and Dwight Way. Beyond lay the deep blue bay scattered with its tiny islands that were not really tiny at all, and on its far shore stood San Francisco in minute, heaped-up blocks of white. Directly opposite her lay the Golden Gate, where the bay flowed into the Pacific, with San Francisco on the southern side of the Gate and the green-furred hills of Marin County swelling away to the north. Now Julia could see what Uncle Phil meant by the shape of an Indian maiden lying asleep along the tops of the mountains in Marin County, where groves of redwoods stood at the foot of Mount Tamalpais.

She snuffed the fresh, delicious smell of new lumber mingled with eucalyptus, for here too, as down at the brown bungalow, the big trees clattered their sickle leaves, shapes that seemed cut from thin silvery-green leather already blowing in drifts across the floors. In a ravine that dropped away abruptly below the living room windows, the trees grew thick in a little forest. Fun to play down there — no one could ever find you if you were Indian-still — and the cats could go hunting. When she knelt at the brink of the floor to peer over, she discovered it was so steep and deep that her stomach flopped: the jungle of branches and leaves kept you from knowing just how many feet down it might —

In one dizzying motion she was suddenly hooked up by an arm that went round her and snatched her back from the edge.

"Never do that —" Uncle Phil's voice shook and his pale gray-green eyes blazed. His lips were set in a curious shape. A piece of his thinning hair stood up at an angle.

"Never, in this house, hang over the edge like that again, kneeling and leaning over. You could have been —"

At his words, his tone, something blazed through Julia as though a hot knife had struck. She snatched herself away and stared up at his face, her own face burning.

"Leave me alone," she shot at him fiercely. "You leave me alone. Don't you ever tell me what to do — don't you *touch* me — you're not my father —" and she turned and raced out of the room, along a passage, out the front, around the house and down an embankment at the side. The forest, she thought, the little forest, and made for it, sliding down the side of the ravine at the back, then crouching in the cool, flickering shade. She listened. But no sound came from up there where they must be standing looking down on the eucalyptus grove, watching to see what she would do, her mother furious and thinking she should be called up to apologize.

But — had she really been going over? She couldn't remember, only looking down, feeling sick and giddy, feeling her stomach turn at sight of the drop, and she could hear even now (so that it must have happened) a cry that could only have been her mother's. She put her hands to her face and it was still burning, and now the whole of her body burned. She got up and slipped over to where she could peer up at the house without being seen, and there were Greg and her mother and Uncle Phil standing together with their backs to her, and Uncle Phil was gesturing, explaining something about a room over on the other corner, and Greg walked off a little way and waved an arm around. Then her mother laughed, blithe and careless. And she, Julia, might have been killed!

Well, if they wanted her, they could shout for her. She stood watching a moment longer and when they moved away and disappeared, she turned and went deeper into the grove.

Chapter Seven

She knelt and picked up several of the fallen leaves and
made a little fan of them, arranging them by colors from
silvery to deeper green, green paling to pink, to reddish
pink, to a certain soft faded red that brought to her mind,
for some reason, the sight of Mrs. Moore's bedroom. Yes,
she remembered. These were the colors of her bedroom:
the gold and silver and gray-green in the wallpaper like
a grove of trees with sun falling through interlacing
branches, the silver-green of the carpet the exact shade of
the silver-green leaf in her hand, and the faded pinkish red
of the silk quilt on her bed the color of the faded rosy-red
one. Was it because Rhiannon Moore so loved the eucalyptus trees that she wanted their colors around her in her
bedroom?

Someday, thought Julia, and she slipped the leaves into her coat pocket in case she couldn't find that exact shade of red in the driveway at home, someday I'm going to have a bedroom with those colors, and a fireplace like Mrs. Moore's, so that when I'm sick I can lie there and watch the fire. Golly, it'd be worth being sick if you could have all your books and stuff around you and a fire going on a cold, rainy day with the other kids sloshing home from school and someone coming in with a tray — hot chocolate and peanut butter sandwiches just to keep going on till dinnertime. But she was *never* sick, only gashed up or bruised or both, the way she'd been after the telephonepole crash. "My sturdy pony," her mother called her. And she was built like that — squarish and firm and solid.

"Haven't you ever seen eucalyptus leaves before?"

Julia's head went up, and there to her astonishment, a short way off in deep shadow with a notebook in her lap and some papers and magazines at her side, sat crosslegged a girl of about Julia's age. No older, thought Julia. She sat there relaxed, leaning against the great trunk of a mammoth tree. And she was smiling a little, as a grown-up would, watching a child. Whereupon at once Julia felt uncomfortably young and her face burned again. How old would she be before it never did grow hot like this, simply at some turn of events or because of a look! And between one breath and the next she tried to picture herself as she must have appeared to the girl, fiddling around with leaves: had she been making faces or talking out loud? She shrugged and her eyebrows went up.

85

"Of course I've seen them, millions of times. Who hasn't? We have them everywhere at home. But it was a certain color I wanted — an absolutely certain shade, because of a friend of mine."

"Oh — I see." They studied one another. The girl's face was round, though she herself was not in the least fat; slim, rather. Her eyes were smallish, and her nose too, and even her mouth was smaller than most. She had very thick perfectly straight brown hair that shone where flecks of sunlight struck it, and it was drawn back into what was probably a clasp. She was unusual-looking, Julia thought, in exactly the opposite way Greg was, with his great Egyptian eyes and his beak of a nose and wide mouth. But this girl, despite the smallness of her features, was not in the least doll-faced. She contemplated Julia with great gravity, with a kind of still, watching attentiveness, and Julia herself felt suddenly quiet, no longer ruffled and uneasy like a startled partridge, being aware as she was of the friendly curiosity and interest communicated from those studying eyes. "I see," the girl said again. "Is that your house? Are you going to live up there?"

Julia pulled her mouth down in complete disdain.

"I should say *not*. It belongs to a friend of my mother's — it hasn't anything at all to do with us, my mother and Greg and me. Greg's my brother. He's about your age. How old are you?"

"Fourteen and a half."

"So's Greg. But in some ways you'd never think it. I mean, he says such *old* things sometimes, then other times

86

you don't know what to make of him, but it's because he has thoughts in his head that nobody can guess at. He's like my mother in that way — he just begins talking and you know he's saying his thoughts out loud and you can't connect. But I can follow my mother's thoughts. If she says something peculiar, I can usually hitch it up, even if it's from the day before because I know her so well. It's a kind of game. But I can't do that with Greg very often, because he knows things my mother and I don't — historical things. That's what he loves, history. But sometimes you'd think he wasn't all there."

The girl's face had filled with amusement; her eyes shone. She had begun smiling as she listened and her smile broadened, she folded her hand and pressed it against her mouth and as Julia finished she burst out laughing. Now her cheeks were round as apples on either side of her laughing mouth and her teeth shone white from out of the pool of shadow. Julia had never heard such a laugh, intoxicating, the kind you would try to call back by saying something funny just for the pleasure of hearing it again. Julia, too, had to burst out laughing and then, at length, when their amusement had settled:

"What are you doing? Homework?"

"No, it's poetry."

Julia stared at her, becoming perfectly still. "You mean — your *own* poetry?"

"Yes, writing it. My own. Shouldn't I be?" The girl was teasing.

Julia had nothing to say for a moment, so strongly she felt this meeting was fated.

"I write too," she announced presently in a hushed voice. "Poetry sometimes, but mostly stories. Where do you send yours? I send mine to the Young Writers' Page."

"Oh, yes — I used to, ages ago. Now I send them to *St. Nicholas.*" The girl picked up one of the two magazines she had with her, flipped it open and handed it to Julia without moving, and Julia had to get up, brush off her knees and go and get it. She sank down, her eyes eagerly searching the page.

"But which is — I don't even know your name."

"Leslie Vaughan Carlson. It's that one —" and the narrow brown hand pointed. "The one at the bottom — there. It's a sonnet."

Julia read with appalled concentration. The poem was called "The Substitute."

I had no need of any light to tell
Me it was Death breathed softly in my ear.
Clearly, as when one waits within a spell,
I heard a drop of rain fall like a tear.
And I, aged cynic, who to morning woke
Weary and gray, who did not really care
For life, grinned when Death beckoned and spoke —
Slipped from his side and left him standing there.

Gently I pressed against my chamber door
And, when it gave, I saw the lighted hall

Stretched high and far, and on the gleaming floor
A woman stood, so young and fair and tall.
Death led her by the hand. The rain fell down.
She only looked at me, but made no sound . . .

Julia read it once, then again, then closed the magazine
and lifted it to her chest with her arms crossed over it just
the way she had carried her story to the mailbox. She gazed
at Leslie.

"You said you're fourteen."

"Yes —"

Julia swallowed. "I'm never going to write another
poem as long as I live."

"Oh, rubbish! It isn't very good. A poem should be like
a bird, Mrs. Reynolds says — she's my English teacher —
flying, but you can't really figure out how. And this, anybody could —"

"I couldn't!" said Julia fervently. "*I* couldn't, and I
think it's — it's —"

"No. You see, I've used words in an ordinary way. I
mean words like 'weary' and 'gray' and 'stretched' and
'gleaming.' I didn't notice this until I sent the poem in.
I didn't show either my father or Mrs. Reynolds until it
was too late because I wanted to surprise them, and then
my father pointed it out, and of course I saw. I did struggle with 'stretched' before I sent it in, but even now I
can't get the right word. Something's got to come that you
could never just sit and coldly *think* of, and it isn't the
word itself so much as what you make it mean, or at least

89

what the poem makes it mean, Dad says. Oh, well, I can see now — the whole darned thing's not much."

"But Mrs. Reynolds and your parents — don't they think your poetry's good?"

Leslie made an odd, quick face.

"You should hear my mother! That's why I had to laugh when you were telling about Greg. I know all about *that,* how I sound so old, beyond my years. My mother's absolutely fatuous, but not Dad. I've always read poetry, Yeats and Wordsworth and Emily Dickinson — you should read *her!* — ever since my father first saw I wanted to write it and he gave me his books to read. He says I'm doing fairly well considering my age, but I get tired of that. No poem's ever good — just good for my age. He says I probably won't write anything that could be called poetry until I'm seventeen or eighteen, if then — at least he hopes I won't."

"But that's years! Why does he hope that?"

"Because he says child prodigies hardly ever amount to anything, just peter out and are miserably unhappy because they can't write poetry or novels, or whatever, that are worth publishing any more. That would be terrible," said Leslie with passion. "I don't know how I'd live. Anyway, I'm no child prodigy — far from it, even though my mother thinks I am — and I *am* going to be a poet."

"Oh, I know," said Julia. "I know you are." She opened *St. Nicholas* again and read the other poems on the page. "Yours is much, much the best," she said when she'd finished. "It's better than any of them."

"Why? Because it rhymes?"

"I don't know — I just like it best."

"Mrs. Reynolds says that a real poet should be able to write any form, so I've been trying them all, but I'm working now on an unrhymed one. Would you like to show me yours sometime?"

"I wouldn't ever," said Julia, "not in a million years. But I'll bring my new story up — or maybe you'll see it in the paper." At this, she remembered Kathryn Penhallow and the letter, and something, some prop, some support, that had slipped from under her during the last few minutes, was restored. She hadn't realized until this moment what a hollowness had opened inside of her because of Leslie's poem compared with everything — anything — she herself had ever written. "Do you know Mrs. Penhallow, the editor of the Young Writers' Page?"

"She's a very good friend of ours. Do you?"

"Well, she's written to me. I sent her a story and she wants me to come and see her about it. I don't know why."

The expression on Leslie's face was balm and delight.

"*That's* int'resting. She wouldn't ask you to come just for nothing. She's got too much to do, and then she's not very well. Tell me everything after you've been. The Penhallows live right over there —" Leslie pointed beyond the new house — "a couple of blocks over. Come by here on your way home, why not?"

"Ju-*lia!*" Neither of them moved.

"That's mother." And the warmth fled from wherever it had been inside of her and apprehension took its place. Here she was, hidden and happy and at peace, talking about what meant most to her. Out there her face would be studied and she would be made to apologize.

"Julia?" There was an anxious, rising note on the last syllable. Julia got up.

"I wish I could show my mother your poem. She likes poetry. She made up a funny one not very long ago, just made it up while we were walking along, then wrote it all down when we got home. Only she says it's not a poem."

Leslie drew a paper from her notebook.

"Here's a copy of mine. It has one or two words crossed out because I was trying to improve it, but it's all there. You can have it if you want."

"*Ju* — lia!" Mrs. Redfern was getting irked and impatient.

Julia folded Leslie's poem with deliberation and put it in her pocket with the leaves, then ran to the edge of the grove and looked up. Her mother stood at the brink of the living room floor where Uncle Phil had snatched her back, and he and Greg stood behind.

"I'm coming," said Julia quietly. "I've met someone. We've been talking. Her name's Leslie Vaughan Carlson and she's a poet." Julia turned to call her but Leslie had already got up and was some distance away. She raised her arm and disappeared among the trees.

"Regards to Greg, the wonder boy," floated back a mocking voice.

Julia, having muttered "I'm sorry" in scarcely audible tones while staring at the sidewalk — at which Uncle Phil

waved a hand back and forth saying "Forget it, forget it!"
— got into the back seat with Greg, her fingers curled
round the poem in her pocket.

"— Dr. Carlson's daughter," Uncle Phil was saying.
He started up and they rounded the corner onto the street
above. "That's where they live." All heads turned toward
a large white saltbox house on the right, whose rear garden
extended downhill along the lower boundary of Uncle
Phil's property. "He teaches at the university — literature.
English or French, or maybe it's both. An eccentric man,
quite brilliant. His students, I've heard, say there's no one
even begins to compare with him when it comes to —"

But Julia ceased to listen. She was not in the least interested in Leslie's father, only in Leslie, and she was cogi-
tating whether or not to show everybody the sonnet. She
drew it forth, unfolded it and read it over again with sadness mingled with a strange pride. She felt oddly posses-
sive about it, and yet at the same time hurt by it. And it
was because of Leslie's youth: if only she'd been sixteen —
or even fifteen! But she was not; she was fourteen and a
half. Presently Julia glanced at Greg, who seemed to be
thinking of nothing, whistling his plaintive little tune and
twiddling his fingers on his knees. She handed him the
poem and watched his profile intently as he read, but his
expression did not change. Then he gave an exclamation.

"How old is this child?"

"Your age. Are *you* a child?" demanded Julia.

Greg gravely held up a hand. "Blessings," he said.
"Peace. I am not a child. She is not a child. Mom!" he

called. "Did you know? Jule's new friend, at fourteen, is an aged cynic."

They were seated round a pool of polished linen. There were flowers in the center of the table and a little lamp that cast a bloom of light against the backs of four menus. It was green dusk outside and in the corners of the long, glassed-in room. Murmurings rose from the other tables. Occasionally a laugh was tossed up, bass boom or chink of crystal. Waiters with small white towels over their arms stood watching or moved discreetly in and out behind chairs. Nothing could have been more perfect, Julia decided; all, all, was absolutely as she would have wished it. And her mind was at rest, for she had chosen. She laid down the large folded card.

Greg, however, was torn, being unable to settle either on trout, which he remembered as the food of paradise from some long ago camping trip, or on the *boeuf bourguignon,* which sounded elegant, as if he might never have the chance of choosing it again for years and years. "Still, what if it tasted weird," he ruminated aloud, "fixed up with wine and mushrooms and stuff like that, and this golden opportunity laid waste forever!"

"Honestly!" said Julia, though as a matter of fact she had never minded the way he talked, his elevated style. It tickled her. He was like no one else she knew: never in the least troubled at being teased or thought odd. And the strange thing was that girls acted silly because of him, but

94

he paid them not the slightest attention or else answered as if he were their grandfather.

> *Darling adorable,*
> *We love you most horrible —*

they would call after him in the street to try to discomfit him. And he would turn and graciously acknowledge their attentions. "Thank you, ladies, thank you. You are most kind!" in that dry, ironic tone of his, and they didn't know what to make of him. He was hopeless. All the same, they still called after him; they still tried to make him choose one of them in a typical, average, awkward way they could understand. But if there was one thing Greg wasn't, it was typical and average and awkward.

"Don't even begin to expect, Greg," said Uncle Phil, "that hotel trout will remind you of trout caught in a mountain stream and cooked right afterward over a camp-fire."

Julia hunched, round-shouldered, with her hands dug between her knees, feeling peaceful and staring out through the tops of boughs at the lights of Berkeley laid beneath and of San Francisco shimmering as if alive in the far darkness. As for her mother, she seemed exceeding gay.

> *Then sigh not so, but let them go,*
> *And be ye blithe and bonny,*
> *Converting all your sounds of woe*
> *Into "Hey nonny, nonny!"*

she sang under breath as she studied the menu. Julia smiled to herself. My, but wouldn't they be surprised when she gave her order, steak being hideously expensive. She could hardly wait, quite safe and absolutely sure of herself. Uncle Phil had said this was to be a celebration and that they could have whatever they wanted. That was what he'd said: anything. Yes, definitely steak.

"Well," said Uncle Phil when the waiter stepped from the shadows and bent attentively, his little pad and pencil ready. "It seems it'll be the *boeuf bourguignon* all round, apparently. That is, what about you, Julia?"

"I believe I'll have the New York steak," Julia announced with dignity as though she'd just arrived at this decision.

Her mother leaned forward.

"I see," said the waiter. "And how would the young lady prefer her steak? Medium, rare — or possibly —?"

"Neither," said Mrs. Redfern. She leaned closer for privacy. "Julia, there's chicken —"

"I loathe and detest chicken and you know it," said Julia in a clear voice, brushing aside privacy as if it were a fly. "I *said* a New York steak. Uncle Phil said —"

"Celia." Uncle Phil laid a hand on Mrs. Redfern's arm. "Celia, I *did* say. I promised they could have anything —"

"Yes, I know. But Julia doesn't happen to like steak. She won't eat it, it would be wasted, and I happen to know why she's chosen it."

"I said a New York steak." Julia's voice shook. Her eyes burned like chips of sharp glass under the lids; her

96

throat tightened and she knew that the uncontrollable curling of the muscles around her mouth meant that she might be about to cry. Well, she wouldn't. Not if she died, she wouldn't. But all this in *front* of everybody!

"Celia —" began Uncle Phil, troubled, uncertain.

"Do you have any other preferences, Julia?" her mother asked in a low, dangerously level voice. Julia did not answer because she couldn't, so fierce was the battle she was fighting with the shape of her mouth. She could only keep looking down at her hands locked together in her lap. "The *bourguignon* for all of us, then." And when the waiter was gone, "I will not see food wasted at that outrageous price. I will not."

"Well, no — but it was the fact of the promise," said Uncle Phil. "I'd wanted this evening to be a —"

"I know, Phil. But not with that kind of joke. And now, if possible, Julia, I'd like us all to be happy."

"You wouldn't treat Greg like this," Julia burst out. "I'm just a scrapegoat, that's what I am —"

All at once her mother's face sparkled.

"Scapegoat, dear. And you know that's not true about Greg. Now cheer up."

*Scape*goat! What kind of a word was *that* — it didn't mean *any*thing. Because she *did* feel scraped, absolutely scraped to the bone, bloodied. And as for cheering up: I hate her. I *hate* her. That One had fooled them. *He'd* held out for the promise, but not her mother. How could you get around that? You couldn't. I do hate her. (But she didn't; it wasn't possible, or only just now.) And I won't eat a bite of food and I won't say a word from now on, not for the whole evening. I just won't be here — I mean I'll act as if I'm not — and there won't be a thing they can do. I'll build a wall around myself. She stole a quick glance upward at That One, who was listening to her mother with his head a little on one side while he played with a piece of bread. But he still looked troubled and unhappy, listening, but maybe thinking of something else at the same time. His eyes turned to her and at once she looked down.

She remembered sharply a scene from when she was six. She had been teasing the cat and her father said, "If you touch that cat once more, I'll smack you." And she *had* touched the cat once more, teased it, pulled its tail, and her father caught her up and turned her over his knee and spanked her good and hard. And she had never teased that cat again.

But Uncle Phil! She remembered his voice shaking up at the new house. And if she'd talked to her father the way she'd talked to him, he would have whaled her. But of course Uncle Phil wasn't her father. All the same he was silly. He wasn't strong, he wasn't the boss. He was anxious and uncertain about the steak. *He* hadn't said, "Of course Julia must have the steak. There's no question. I keep my promises." Either that, or in an easy sort of voice, "Oh, come on now, Julia — if you hate steak, why not get something you'll like? Let's see here —" She'd bet that's what her father would've done. But oh, no, not That One, not with her mother saying no. She stole another glance at him and observed his rather roundish head with its thinning hair, his gray-green eyes and gentle, thin lips. Funny, she'd never thought much about Uncle Phil before. He was always just there, always around. Why was she, now, moved to study him so closely? She didn't know. She'd never even thought enough about him in her life before the affair of the play last week to ever dislike him or be scornful of him. But now she *saw* him and she was filled with derision. He wasn't dark and rich-looking like her father. Her father had had thick hair and dark eyes, deep-set, with thick eyebrows. Uncle Phil was pale compared to her father, compared to Greg even. Her father had been like a raven. Uncle Phil's roundish head seemed comical somehow compared to her father's handsomely shaped one. She looked at Uncle Phil's hand, which she'd never noticed before, and saw that it was squarish with square, evenly cut nails. Her father's fingers had been long and clever like Greg's, and she had liked the dark hairs on the back of them and how fine the hand had looked with its heavy ring and a gold wristwatch to set it off.

The salad came and Julia forgot, in a keen hunger born of the dregs of her anger, that she had not been going to eat. Uncle Phil's *nothing* compared to my father, she was thinking, when all at once:

"What's going on in that head of yours, Julia?" At first she didn't really hear, so intense was her thought, so clear the image of that photograph of her father on her desk at home. Then the words sifted in. It was Uncle Phil asking and she grinned to herself.

"You'd be surprised," she said, and gave a wicked chuckle, then forked up a long tail of cut lettuce and put back her head to drop it in slowly, a bit at a time, as if it had been spaghetti. But as her head came up, she saw her mother's ominous expression and quickly she twirled her fork and whisked the lettuce into her mouth with a neat little flick before Mrs. Redfern could say so much as a word.

"Golly, 'apprehensive'!" said Greg suddenly, out of nothing that connected with what they had been talking about on the way home, very late, after the picture show, with Julia dozing beside him. "Now, that's a funny thing. Listen, everybody. When you apprehend something, you *know* it. In other words, you catch on, you have a piece of knowledge. And when you apprehend a villain, you catch him. So you know him better, because you *have* him."

"That's right," said Uncle Phil.

"But if you're apprehensive, it's because you *don't* have knowledge you should have. You're scared in an anxious way because you don't know all you should know. It's the very opposite. Well — that's not very clear, I guess, but you see what I mean —"

I see, thought Julia.

"Yes. Yes, I do, Greg," said his mother, and she twisted round in the front seat to face him. "You mean you could be in a state of apprehension, meaning that you're in a state of knowing —"

"And in a state of apprehension when you *don't* know something," finished Uncle Phil, "when you're in a state of *not* knowing."

"That's it, that's it!" exulted Greg. "Boy, that's it exactly! It's just funny the way some words turn out when you really think about them."

"Well, funny, I suppose. Curious, at any rate," said Uncle Phil. Then, after a silence, "But in another way, not so funny. I apprehend many things, and because of them I'm apprehensive."

"Poor Phil," said Mrs. Redfern, and she seemed really to mean it. But why? wondered Julia. What was he apprehensive *about?*

Julia lay in her bed, not sleepy now but wide awake. Her light was out, the moon was sending a shaft of silver swimming across the bed through the skylight. Her cats were up, having run in with little welcoming cries from the cool June darkness. Sandy was stretched at her side purring, and Gretchy was mounded on her chest, purring and trying to knead as she crouched, thus rocking from side to side and looking as silly as it is possible for a cat to look. Julia stroked Sandy with one hand and Gretchy with the other, she herself as soothed and contented and peaceful as the cats. Yes, but —

"Mother," she called.

"Yes, Julia?" Mrs. Redfern was in the next room, brushing and brushing her long chestnut hair by the light of a small lamp on her dressing table, a light that penetrated the darkness of Julia's room only a little and that did not in the least affect the moonlight.

"Did you really read Leslie's poem or just glance at it?"

"I read it, and I think it remarkable. I can't believe it — fourteen!"

"I'm just not anywhere compared to her — or to Greg either, am I? I'm just nothing."

"What nonsense. You're younger than Leslie, and who knows what you'll do when you're fourteen. As for Greg, you're entirely different. He's thoughtful, logical, more interested in ideas and in putting them together to make something new, at least for himself. You're thoughtful, too, in a way, but more emotional, more intuitive than Greg."

"But Greg liked Leslie's poem. He knew it was good."

"Oh, yes. Greg has many sides."

"Is that the way Leslie is — like me, I mean?"

"I imagine so. I gather so from her poem."

"And what's *Addie?*" There was a tingle of amusement in Julia's voice.

Her mother, Julia could tell, had stopped brushing her hair. And there she was, suddenly, in her nightgown and robe with her hair down her back and the hairbrush in her hand, standing silhouetted in the doorway.

"Don't you ever let me hear you being scornful of Addie Kellerman. She has qualities you don't have and may never have, and don't you forget it."

Julia stared at her mother in utter astonishment.

"Well, *what,* for instance — *what?*" she demanded hotly.

"For one thing, Addie pierces to the heart. She never fools herself, even at her age. But you dramatize. And for the sake of your drama, you cover over what you don't like — or don't need for your story, of which you're always the center."

Julia thought this over.

"You said — 'and may never have.' Qualities, that is. But how do *you* know? And I don't really fool myself. I know what's underneath my story."

"Do you, Julia? Are you sure? You mean you always know — for instance about putting that photograph of your father on your desk just lately?"

Julia hunched up one of her shoulders and dug her chin into it, then picked up Gretchy and buried her face in the soft fur that smelled of damp grass and the cool night air.

"Addie never makes up stories. She couldn't. And I meant — when I think of what Leslie can do and what she's interested in compared with Addie."

"What difference does that make?" said her mother with passion. "You just think about Addie herself. What's more, she's only your age. And those two — Addie and Leslie — are from entirely different backgrounds. Oh, when I think of that child coming from the Kellerman house and that father of hers — don't you ever say one word to hurt Addie Kellerman."

"All *right* — whoever *said* I'm going to?"

"Promise me, Julia!" Her mother stood there, and Julia could feel her fiery intensity and concentration. She tried to resist it, to refuse any sort of answer, but it was not possible.

"I promise," she muttered under her breath, puzzled and rebellious. *This* wasn't the sort of conversation she'd wanted or expected at all!

Chapter Eight

Addie and Julia sat at the big table in front of the oak tree window in a comfortable silence (at least Julia's silence was comfortable), with glasses of milk in front of them and in their hands almost unbelievably thick slices of bread spread lavishly with butter and sugar. Each slice was disappearing with such rapidity that without doubt two more would have to be cut and spread in another minute or so. The girls had walked home from school together and Julia had told Addie the whole of yesterday's events, a richly dramatic tale the way Julia related it, to which Addie had listened with engrossed attention. As she ate, she read Leslie's poem. Now she laid it down without comment, looked at Julia for a second or two, her tongue exploring for stray sugar, then went on eating. She finished her slice, took a long drink of milk, and sat staring straight ahead at the trunk of the oak. She seemed sunk in solemnity, with a white milk moustache tilted up on either side of her upper lip. She was relaxed, her hands folded on her stomach, her feet swinging and her heels banging rhythmically against the legs of her chair.

"Well, then, I guess," she said after a while, "Leslie'll be your best friend from now on and not me."

Julia's eyes widened; she looked down and made a little careful design in the sugar on her plate. This was what her mother had meant last night — Addie's way of going right to the heart of a matter without the least warning; maybe saying something, as she had now, that you didn't know you knew but that made you discover you'd had this idea, whatever it might be, nestled away in the back of your mind all along.

She wiped her mouth on the back of her hand.

"*How* could I have Leslie for a best friend when I don't even really know her and she's older than me and lives way up there in the hills?" Without asking Addie if she wanted any more, because there was no need, Julia went out and fixed two more slices and brought them in. With pensive gravity Addie chewed and stared at the oak tree.

"Anyway," she said, swallowing, "I'll have Paul this summer. He'll be here — at least for a while. So that'll be fun."

"Well, so'll *I* be here — and for a heck of a lot longer than a while," cried Julia with such vehemence that it made her burp loudly and abruptly and they had to laugh and laugh until they choked and their faces got red. When their mirth died, Addie looked around.

"Are you rich?" she asked suddenly.

"*Rich!*" exclaimed Julia. The notion was preposterous, and she was about to tell Addie exactly why it was when a little subtle turn of feeling came over her. "Well, I don't know," she said airily. "Maybe."

"What I mean is," said Addie, "this room is pretty. I like the colors, and the rug — it's thick — and the way the furniture is all sort of dark and smooth, and your curtains — gold, I guess, like the walls." They were a pale, grayed yellow. "I'm going to have a room just like it someday, with branches put into vases the way your mother does. And I'm going to have a table like this." She stroked her finger lightly across the surface that Mrs. Redfern polished once a week and upon which no one — *no one* — could do his homework or any writing at all without first putting down a magazine. "Julia, listen!" Addie's gray eyes suddenly shone with excitement. "I've got an idea. You know how ugly our big old house is —"

"It sure is," agreed Julia heartily. She'd never really thought much about it one way or the other — it was just Addie's house — but she had heard Mrs. Kellerman say more than once that it was ugly. It was a barn of a place, all worn and hollow and echoing, a weathered tan inside and out. Colored glass in the front door, sending down diamonds of blood red, seaweed green, mustard yellow and cold blue, made the shadowed hall seem haunted somehow, melancholy, for it was never direct sunlight that shone through, but reflected light from the confines of the big front veranda.

Bare boards resounded as feet clumped or ran up and down stairs, across the uncarpeted hall and into the big high-ceilinged kitchen. Here the walls were naked laths between which squeezes of plaster had pressed forth and solidified and become dusty and yellow. Never, in all these years, had the walls even begun to be finished, though behind the sink there was tar paper partway up. A naked bulb hung on a cord directly over the vast, hacked dining table of fumed oak where the Kellermans ate all their meals and where Addie and Ken and Julia had played absorbed games of Flinch after dinner, times without number, yelling and pounding on the table in their wild excitement. Tall uncurtained windows let in floods of sun or, on gray days or late afternoons, a stern coldness. At night, dark green blinds were pulled down and little old Gram worked with ferocious energy between the table and Black Marya (Mar-eye-a), the children's name for the enormous black wood-burning stove with its clanking lids. It didn't matter what anybody was talking about at the Kellermans' at mealtime; if Grammy wanted to cut in about food, she just did and she kept on doing it until she was satisfied. You could tell the pattern of her duties in the kitchen, thirty years or more of them, from the brown paths on the linoleum.

"Why can't we have new linoleum?" Addie's mother would complain. "Why can't we have kitchen curtains?" But it was Gram's house, and Addie's mother, even though she was the one who worked to earn them all a living, was only a daughter-in-law and not much liked at that. At least so Julia gathered from various remarks Gram had made.

"More washin' to do," Gram would say. "I've got enough. Jus' cut off the light, curtains would. Never did like curtains in a kitchen." And that was the end of it.

"But why doesn't your father *fix* the kitchen?" Julia asked, echoing a question her own mother had often puzzled over.

"Because he never does anything, that's why," said Addie fiercely. "And Grammy won't ask him. Mom's been at him to do something about it, and about the front yard and the back because Paul and Aunt Kit and Uncle Norm are coming, and Aunt Kit's her sister and she's cried about it, it makes her so sick to think what *they'll* think, though anyway they'll be staying up at the Piedmont and only Paul'll stay with us. But she can't stand the idea of their coming at all now she knows nothing's going to be any diff'rent. And this makes my father mad, and then he begins drinking and he gets mean — he's so mean to Kenny sometimes you wouldn't believe it, and it's because Mom's after him. But he's *got* all day — wouldn't you think he'd do *some*thing?" Addie's eyes blazed as she stared off for a minute, then she turned back to Julia again. "But I was thinking — why couldn't I get branches and put them in vases in the living room and surprise Mom, just to show her how it could look the day Aunt Kit and Uncle Norm and Paul come? I'll bet it'd help. Don't you think it'd help?" she demanded of Julia with piercing anxiety.

"Yes, it would," said Julia. "And we'll get the stuff out of my backyard because you don't have anything. Not that would do, anyway."

After a deafening clatter, she found her mother's sawtooth bread knife in the kitchen drawer, the knife Mrs. Redfern treasured because she could cut both bread and meat loaf so beautifully straight with it, but with no other, and away they streamed out the back door. Scotch broom, her mother said the big bushes were, with the sweet-smelling yellow blossoms like bonnets where the bees were busy working, and the other beyond was mirror plant with shiny dark green leaves. Julia hacked away with vigor until she had a big mound, then tossed the bread knife down among the rose bushes.

"I'd pick some roses but I don't think Mrs. de Rizzio would like it, and she's not home to ask. She always picks those herself and gives Mom some. That way we know she wants to be the one to do it. Here, you take half the branches and I'll take half. Got any vases?"

Fifteen minutes later they had dug out a tall cut-glass vase from the back of a crowded closet in the bedroom where Addie and Kenny and their mother slept, and had found a big ironstone pitcher and a smaller white enamel one down in the pots and pans cupboard under the kitchen sink. Now they were in the living room and, to Julia's frustrated surprise, Addie had her mirror plant arranged in the ironstone pitcher in no time and had put it on a little table that stood exactly in the center of three windows that made a bay at the front of the room. Julia struggled with her Scotch broom in the cut-glass vase, but it only looked "flopped," she said. Whereupon Addie came over and worked with it, adjusting the branches by pulling out here and pushing in there again and again until she was satisfied; then she took the vase over to a naked table upon which were always to be found a fat, brassbound photograph album with "Memories" embossed on it in stick letters and beside it a statue of a rather bare lady with a lamb slung over her shoulder. These two objects had never once changed their positions, though Gram dusted once a week, nor was anything else ever put on that table. Addie stood the vase in the center, shoving the album and statue to one side. Then she slid the rest of the broom into the enamel pitcher, tweaked it about, stepped back, stepped forward, tweaked and tweaked again and finally got up on the piano bench and put the pitcher on top of the piano. Now she went over to the hall door and took in the whole effect.

"Julie, come and look." She was alight with pleasure. You couldn't really do much about this narrow room with its thin, stubbed rug, its butcher paper walls with one small picture hung very high up under the molding (there had used to be one near the piano of Mr. and Mrs. Kellerman when they were first married, but it had disappeared and now there was a light place there), its stiff chairs put stiffly about and its coarse lace curtains. No one ever came here, though Addie used to when she practiced her pieces faithfully every afternoon, but did not now because there was no more money for piano lessons. All was comfortless. Yet, with something green and graceful in it, the touches of yellow, the room *was* changed — a little. Addie was overcome. "Wait till Mom sees," she said reverently. "Oh, Julie, what d'you s'pose she'll say? Oh, *I* know!" She grabbed Julia's arm in fingers tense and strong with excitement. "Let's clean off the hall table and put the rest of the yellow stuff in the coffeepot. It needs something out here and she'll see it the minute she comes in —"

She turned and began sweeping everything off: Kenny's jacket and her own, a pile of magazines, innumerable anonymous litter, and finally Grammy's rusty black hat which she wore to the market every day of her life and which Addie now tossed on the floor with the other things. There was a sound overhead; Julia looked up — and there was Gram gazing at them from the stair landing.

"Whut're you doin'?" she demanded in her high, old woman's voice. "Whut've you two been up to in my livin' room?"

"Grammy, Grammy!" cried Addie, hopping. "Come and look — it's beautiful — you'll never guess —"

Gram whipped down and stood at the door. Her little black eyes in their triangular folds of flesh went here — there — and there. Then she marched across to the big table and snatched up the cut-glass vase, tore out the branches, put the vase on the floor and got the ironstone pitcher from the little table up front and did the same thing. Then she came back and shoved the greenery into

Julia's arms, hopped up on the piano bench, quick as a squirrel, and got down the enamel pitcher. Meanwhile Addie was crying out in anguish and darting about in her wake making futile efforts to stop the movements of those wiry, determined arms.

"Grammy — no! It was so hard to fix them right — you're *ruining* everything, and it was so beautiful. Julie and I did it for Mom, to show her — *don't* Grammy — oh, *please* don't —"

But Gram never stopped once, her mouth thin, her eyes snapping; she never paid the slightest attention, but simply brushed Addie aside. And now with her apron she was scrubbing at the top of the photograph album where drops of water must have splashed on it from her angry gestures with the branches. She glared up at them.

"You get your soppy, dirty stuff outa this room and don't you ever put that trash in here again. Leaves and mess everyplace! And that's my cut-glass vase — where's it been? A weddin' present, that was — and this album — all these years, not one spot!"

"Well, but you don't ever *use* it," sobbed Addie, "the vase, I mean. Never any flowers — never anything in this horrible old house —"

" 'Tain't horrible!" cried Gram in a fury, facing them now with the vase clasped against her flat chest. "It's my house, that your gran'pa built hisself, every stick. That's all I ever hear outa your ma — this ugly house. Well, if she thinks it's so all-fired ugly, why's she stay? Nobody's askin' her!"

Addie turned and pounded upstairs, and Julia heard the bedroom door slam, the key turn, and the twangle and creak of springs as Addie flung herself across the bed. Gram, without another word, went out with the two pitchers and the vase, leaving Julia standing there simmering. She would stay, and she would tell Addie's mother just exactly what had happened. Not fair! All that work for nothing, and there *wasn't* any mess — it was Gram who'd made the mess. She and Addie's father: those two together were against Addie and Kenny and Mrs. Kellerman.

Julia sat herself down in one of the stiff chairs to go over the whole thing furiously in her mind, and to plan exactly what she would say to Mrs. Kellerman. Thoughtfully her glance strayed to the piano and the longer she studied it the more beguiled she became until at last she went to it, sank onto the piano stool, put her hands on the keys, and then all thought of Addie slipped right out of her head. Now that she herself no longer took lessons (she wanted to write far more than she wanted to play, she'd told her mother, so why waste the money?), Mrs. de Rizzio had asked her please not to touch the piano that stood in a dark corner of the de Rizzios' living room where the painting of the sinking ship was, because Julia's wild vigor tried her nerves so and the wet apple cores she left along the top of the turned back cover marked it. Julia loved chords, especially with the pedal down so that you got a rich, thunderous, reverberant booming when you played the bass end. Sounding chords made her feel that she was actually performing like a real pianist, like Mrs.

Moore, so that now as she sat at the Kellermans' piano, she completely forgot her surroundings and Addie and what Grammy had done, and just let herself go. Oh, it was splendid! She flung back her head, stared off deeply, raptly, into the distance and lifted her hands high, brought them down with abandon, black keys, white keys, and both together, then bent low over the keyboard to manipulate some difficult little runs —

"What in tarnation's sake is that unholy racket!" screamed Gram, and her appalled face swam into focus.

"It's the *Old Hundred*," replied Julia loftily, finishing off her run then coming down with a crash on the final chord.

"Well, it sounds like the old Nick to me, and I'd thank ye to stop it an' clear out. Just take that mess o' yours and clear right out o' here this minute. An' it's the *Old Hundredth*, not the *Old Hundred*, an' it never sounded anything like that, I can tell ye!"

Julia got up, not too fast (it never paid to show you were being hustled — not ever), picked up the branches with quiet deliberation and went out onto the veranda, leaving the front door just slightly ajar behind her. She expected Gram to come and slap it to, but she didn't, and by the time Julia had dumped the branches over the side railing and turned and peeked in, Gram had disappeared and could be heard out on the back porch banging something metal with what must have been suppressed rage. Whereupon Julia nipped upstairs and, leaning her head against the bedroom door, rattled the knob.

"It's me, Addie. C'mon over to my house and play." Silence. "Addie?"

"No," said Addie finally in a muffled voice. "You go home. I don't feel like playing. I don't feel like doing anything. I'm just going to stay here till Mom comes, and tell her."

But Julia remained with her head against the door, for now, rejected, she felt herself sliding inexorably into one of those dreaded times when she didn't know what to do with herself. At school, in the midst of boring old arithmetic, at which she was hopeless, she had desired with a sense of tremendous energy and anticipation to run home and work on her story about a fantastical creature whose name had come to her like a gift right in the middle of a test. But then she had seen Addie after school and had begun at once to tell her the tale of Sunday's adventures, and that ruined everything. Telling a story and then playing games or, indeed, just telling a story made you not want to write. Or coming home and playing and then deciding to go and write was no good because your eagerness to write was all drained away and it was too easy to just go on playing. Now she felt scattered, unchanneled, listless. There wouldn't be time to go to the library. If she went home she would read — that would be the only good thing to do, or maybe chop some wood for Mrs. de Rizzio, or go up and see Daddy. Yes, that was what she would do. Suddenly she felt warm and happy, just thinking of Daddy Chandler, and she turned — and there was Mr. Kellerman. There was the gaunt face, the hound dog eyes and the long sad mouth rising toward her out of gloom into shadow.

The Kellermans' upstairs hall was a little dark box made up of Gram's door, always closed and locked when she wasn't on the other side; opposite it, her son's, Mr. Kellerman's; next to his, the bathroom door opening into a narrow oblong like a dim cave where there was a tank high over the toilet with a long chain to pull, and a bathtub encased in wood all scraped and stained; and on the fourth side, the door to Mrs. Kellerman's and Addie's and Ken's room, where Ken had a corner with a couch bed and a curtain to pull across for "his place."

Julia stood flattened. She stared at Mr. Kellerman like a leveret with huge eyes and pulsing heart, planning desperately how she could slip past, but there was no space. He was smiling at her, and the smile sat strangely on his thin jaws. He held out his hand as he stood, finally, in the center of the hall.

"I have something to show you," he said, and reached down and took her hand with firm gentleness and drew her toward his room. "Something funny I think you'll like. You've never been in my room, have you? Addie says you like books —"

"Mr. Kellerman — I have to go. Please let me go. My mother'll be home — I'm supposed to —"

"But it'll only take a minute." They were in his room, and the green blinds were like the kitchen blinds only more cracked and torn. His bed was unmade ("I don't want you nosing in my room," Julia had heard him tell

Gram), his clothes were thrown over a tin trunk, there were hundreds and hundreds of books stacked around on the floor, and on the walls hung big dark old-fashioned paintings of other Kellermans, very stern and thin-lipped, in deep curly gold frames that slanted inward. Still holding her by the hand, he threw up the blinds and got an album like the one on the living room table, sat down and pulled her toward him as though he would have liked her to sit on his knee. But she snatched her hand away and backed toward the door. He gazed at her out of his deep-set sorrowful eyes, his shoulders hunched.

"You don't want to stay. You don't like me either. I don't have any little girl —"

"You do, too. You have Addie —"

"She won't come near me. I have no children —"

"But it's because," cried Julia, and before she could stop herself, what she knew and what she felt rushed out of her, "it's because you hit Kenny and swear at him. It's because you yell. You're mean! Why're you so mean —?" Then horror-stricken at what she'd said, she turned and snatched open the door he'd closed behind them, raced down the stairs as if she expected him on her heels reaching out to clutch her back and, scarcely aware of turning the knob of the front door, pelted across the veranda and down the front steps and along the street. Dimly, sick with fear, she remembered afterwards that someone called after her, and she thought it was probably Gram — or could it have been Addie? But she never stopped once and did not even slow down until she was in her own driveway.

"Child — child, what is it? What on earth is the matter with you?"

Julia stopped in mid-flight and looked up, and there was Rhiannon Moore staring down at her from the bedroom window. Only now did she discover that she had been making queer sobbing exclamations, but at sight of Mrs. Moore she stopped.

"You're home!" She put her hands on her hips and pressed her lips together and narrowed her eyes. "It's that Mr. Kellerman again."

"Come up and tell me," said Rhiannon Moore.

Julia, flying up Mrs. Moore's back steps, banging into the kitchen, thumping upstairs to the second floor, felt herself too rich, too overflowing with all the things she had to tell: about Kathryn Penhallow's letter, about yesterday and almost falling off the new house, and then Leslie and her poem and dinner at the Piedmont, and then today and Addie and Gram and the horror of Mr. Kellerman. Where to break into this wealth; where to begin? Now there was Rhiannon Moore, looking herself again with her thick hair elegantly done up and her eyes clear and her face young the way it had been the night she rescued Julia, and she was sitting on her bed laughing in the midst of the clothes she had been taking out of her suitcase. She held out her arms and Julia ran over and gave her a hug.

Where to begin? "Why, at the beginning!" Mrs. Moore folded herself among her pillows, shoving them around to get comfortable for the telling, and Julia sat cross-legged on the quilt the color of pinkish-red eucalyptus leaves. And when she had worked her way up to the present, to Mr. Kellerman:

"But, do you know, I feel a certain amount of sympathy for that man," said Rhiannon Moore. "Up to a point, that is — only up to a point. Sympathy for Addie, naturally, and Ken — yes, and their mother. The old lady, of course, can take care of herself. In a way, Addie rather reminds me of her, in her acceptance of life. Only Addie'll never blind herself about anyone the way old Mrs. Kellerman blinds herself about her son."

"But why sympathy for Mr. Kellerman," demanded Julia in astonishment.

"Because he's caught, that's why. He drinks because he's failed, and he's failed because he drinks. Of course his mother's always had her little fictions about him since he was a boy — I well remember. Her newest, so I hear from the shopkeepers, is that he suffers a heart condition and so can't be expected to do anything."

Julia considered this, while Mrs. Moore got up from the bed and went on putting her clothes away.

"About the little fictions — you mean stories."

"Yes —"

"That's finding excuses for him."

"I don't imagine," said Mrs. Moore, "that your mother is much of an excuser. I feel this, though I don't know her."

Julia thought of her mother's passion last night about Addie.

"Anyhow," she said, "I'm like Leslie — I'm *going* to be something, maybe not a poet, but a writer, and Addie doesn't feel that way about anything. She'll probably have a whole bunch of kids."

Mrs. Moore turned for a moment and regarded her, only Julia felt that she was not being actually seen and that what Mrs. Moore did see was anything but happy.

"I, too, once had an ambition — as great as my son's," she said, and there was a remoteness in her voice. "But there are other ways of living, let me tell you. And those other ways are not to be brushed indifferently aside, not for anything." She was silent. "You may not write at all, you know," she finished matter-of-factly.

Julia gazed at her in shocked disbelief. She felt betrayed. She felt as if some talisman, some invisible amulet, had been taken from her, something precious and unalterable that had been contained in that midnight talk they had had when they'd first met.

"But I don't understand — you've changed! The other night you said you *knew* I'd be a writer. Why don't you know now?"

"I only want to tell you that just to live with all your senses to the fullest extent, to have a family —"

"To be ordinary, you mean!" cried Julia. "Well, I'm not *going* to be ordinary. That's dis*gu*sting —"

Mrs. Moore suddenly sank into a chair and laughed until the tears came to her eyes while Julia stared at her in bewilderment, not knowing what to think.

"Oh, Julia — 'disgusting'! That's marvelous. It's such a funny word to use, a ridiculous word, and yet I know what you mean. I used to feel that, centuries ago. And now, I can't tell you what happiness I've had in Oren, in his career and his enormous giftedness, far greater than mine. I myself was going to be a concert pianist, and I did play in public for a while, but now all my pleasure is in him. And am I ordinary, is your mother ordinary, is Zoë de Rizzio ordinary?"

"You couldn't be," said Julia. "And my mother — well, she's my mother. But Mrs. de Rizzio was going to be an actress and now all she's got is *The Delsarte Speaker*. Her grandmother was an actress, but Mrs. de Rizzio just gave up and married Mr. de Rizzio and now all that's left is, she stands in the middle of the living room and does Anger, and Despair, and Sorrow, and Hope, and Determination — you know," and Julia slid off the bed and stood with her feet neatly pointed, the left slightly in front of the right, put one hand on her chest and with the other pointed to the floor, her face stern, eyes cast down.

> *"This rock shall fly*
> *From its firm base*
> *As soon as I —*

That's Determination."

"The Delsarte Speaker!" marveled Mrs. Moore. "Why, I remember — oh, I haven't thought of that for years."

But Julia was not to be sidetracked.

"*I'm* never going to hand on my ambition to *any*one — to a bunch of *kids*. I'm going to keep it and work on it and make it grow."

"Then maybe you can manage better than I have done. Maybe you can have it all, your work and everything else besides." Mrs. Moore stood up and held out her hand. "I've been trying to make my own ambition grow lately. That was composing you were listening to all those weeks before the migraine. Even at my age, I may still have written something worth playing for Oren when he arrives. Come along. You shall be my first audience."

They went down the hall and into that room Julia had tried to picture whenever she looked across from her desk to the half-moon windows. But she could never have imagined how the light, strangely intensified by reflection from the de Rizzios' white-painted roof and flooding in down near the floor through pale amber frosted glass, would give this room such a sense of drama, as though it were a stage on which something unforgettable was about to happen. Julia never afterwards forgot the quality of that light, cast up from below onto the ceiling, onto their faces, onto the paneling of the walls and the faded blues and reds of the chairs and couch, onto bronze lamps and other objects that shone softly.

"But what do you mean — at your age?" demanded Julia, going back in her thoughts to what Mrs. Moore had just said while she stood there absorbing all she saw. "You can't be awfully old."

"But I am — very, very old." Mrs. Moore raised the lid of the grand piano and slid the support under it, then sat down and took off her rings, laying them to one side of the music rack. "I am seventy," she said.

Julia was stunned.

"Seventy! But you can't be!" Mrs. Moore might just as well have said that she was one hundred and seventy. "Your hair's dark, even though there's gray in it, and you haven't any wrinkles."

"I expect I'm a witch," said Rhiannon Moore with composure, "or else it's that I can still clap hands and sing, at least in my own way. A great friend of mine, a famous poet now dead, once wrote:

> *An aged man is but a paltry thing,*
> *A tattered coat upon a stick, unless*
> *Soul clap its hands and sing —"*

Then she put her hands on the keys and began to play.

Julia sat at her desk that night while Mrs. Moore, in the music room, worked at her minor-keyed, sad-sounding piece, yet not sad really. Rather it was "a composition of grave contemplation," Mrs. Moore called it. The notes, like drops of water, fell into the silence, each one round, clear, pure. It was a piece written in the Lydian mode, Mrs. Moore had said, which is Greek. And it lingered in the air, it seemed to Julia, as though coming from another time, ancient, other-worldly, as Mrs. Moore worked on it, going back and forth, searching, listening, changing, for she was still not satisfied.

Julia took out her *Book of Strangenesses* and opened it and began to write.

"First of all, I want to put down here that after Mrs. Moore was through playing, I told her how much I would like to hear her son play someday, and she has promised me that when he comes to San Francisco, she will take me if she possibly can. She says she can think of no reason why she shouldn't, but Mother says I am not to build on this because Mrs. Moore is always coming and going.

"Second, I'd never heard of a famous Irish poet by the name of —" here she had to stop and copy off the name on the cover of the thick book that lay in front of her — "William Butler Yeats until Leslie said yesterday that he was one of the people whose poems her father gave her to read. And then today after Mrs. Moore talked about her son, I asked her to say the words over again about soul clap its hands and sing, and she said the whole poem to me, sitting there on the piano bench, and then another poem, and another, and one with something in it about hid his head amid a crowd of stars, and one about an airplane pilot — here it is, I've found it because it's one she marked — An Irish Airman Foresees His Death. And I thought about my father and I told her afterwards that he was killed in the war when his plane went down and that he didn't want to kill anyone, because that was what the poem was about. I told her my mother said he loved flying and Mrs. Moore said she expected he'd felt the lonely impulse of delight, which is in the poem. And I said Mother told me that if he was going to die he'd rather it happened up above the earth and not down in the mud. After that Mrs. Moore went over to the bookshelves and got a book and held it out to me. When I took it she said to look inside the cover and there was what Mr. Yeats had written to her. She said it is one of her treasures because he'd given it to her — his first book of poems — and then she put it back and got another, this big one I have that she had bought, and said that she would trust me to keep it safe and in good order and I knew she meant not to read it while I'm eating an apple or a peanut butter sandwich.

"She marked her favorite poems that she thought I'd like with little pieces of paper. Then I had a strange thought. If I tell Leslie and bring her to meet Mrs. Moore because of Leslie knowing about the poems of Mr. Yeats, then maybe Leslie will be her close friend and not me so much anymore. And this is just like Addie saying, then I guess Leslie will be your best friend now and not me. I don't know if I'll be able to bring Leslie, because Mrs. Moore is my special friend, and I've never known anyone like her.

"I told Mrs. Moore about the eucalyptus leaves and she said that never once has anyone noticed that her room is in the colors of eucalyptus and her wallpaper the color of sun coming through trees. She said no wonder we're friends and that made me think that maybe I could bring Leslie after all because Mrs. Moore and I are firm enough together.

"When I was about to go she asked me if I remembered that she had a letter to mail the night she rescued me from Mr. Kellerman and of course I remembered. I even told her I felt she wasn't sure she should mail it because she put it into the mailbox as if she wanted it to be gone before she could take it back. She shook her head and said Child, child! in an astonished way I thought. Then she told me the letter had been answered and that she is going away for she doesn't know how long to be with the friend she had written to because the friend is not well and for other reasons. She didn't say what they were. But she said that her whole future depends on this visit and asked me to think of her with strong and hopeful thoughts and of course I will. She asked if I would water her houseplants and gave me the front door key and I am to go in and read her books anytime I like. She is going in a few days. I will miss her. I wonder if when I get old I'll be a witch the way she is. I hope so, not all dried up and uninteresting but still working the way she and Daddy Chandler are."

Chapter Nine

The Penhallows' big square brown-shingled house — a
typical Berkeley house — sat in the midst of a wild garden
on the edge of a neighborhood park, so that its background
as well as its own surroundings gave it the air of existing
in a world of its own. Julia went up the brick walk,
heaved into waves here and there by the roots of oaks
pushing up, growing huge and gnarled underground, a
walk whose bricks were green with dampness. Purple and
white cinerarias, ferns, lilies, roses, ivy, lay in beds or crept
over the house and covered old fences. It was a woods,
but a woods where someone had been planting.

She tapped the knocker three times. Faintly she could
hear a typewriter going very fast, like Greg's, and it did
not stop for even a second so she gave the doorbell, so

tarnished that it was scarcely noticeable, a good, hard, long ring. "I'll get it, Glenna," cried a voice. There were footsteps, and the door opened, and Julia gazed fixedly at a worn tweed vest. "It's me — Julia," she announced, not very loud, looking up and up and at length into the surprised face of a very tall thin gray-haired man she thought she might like for a grandfather. Why, this is the way Greg will look someday, came into her head. She would have to tell Greg. "Julia Redfern," she jogged this elderly man. "You remember? I'm expected."

"Of course — how extraordinary — went right out of my head. Do come in — come in! Dear child, I am Dr. Penhallow," and he held out his hand to her and she stepped inside. Pen*hal*low, he had said, not *Pen*hallow, the way she'd been thinking it was. "My wife didn't sleep very well last night, and she's taking a nap. I hate to waken her just yet — ah, but there we are. I hear the little bell. That means she's dressed and ready, so we'll go right up. Glenna —"

"Yes, Dr. Penhallow. Tea, shall it be, now?"

At the hall door there appeared a large, firm, calm-looking woman with thick white hair, that must once have been very dark, wound in a kind of wreath on top of her head. She had a starched apron on and her hands were folded across it. She smiled at Julia, and Julia noticed how beautiful her almost black eyebrows were with her white hair.

"Julia," said Dr. Penhallow, "this is the lady who takes care of us, Mrs. Duncan. Do you take tea?"

"Well," said Julia, "cambric tea — so far."

"Oh, my!" exclaimed Mrs. Duncan. "I haven't heard that for donkey's years, not since I was a child in the Old Country."

"It's what my mother calls it. She's English, and it's what she was allowed to have when she was my age, tea with a lot of milk in it. But I like milk with a lot of tea."

"Well! So then, strong cambric tea for Julia, and strong tea for Dr. and Mrs. Penhallow, and lots of bread and butter and lemon tarts, and possibly for Julia damson plum jam to put on the bread and butter." She sent Julia a look and disappeared.

"And I may tell you," said Dr. Penhallow making for the stairs, "that Mrs. Duncan's bread and tarts are fit for the gods. She makes, of course, as well as tarts and cakes and pies and jam, all her own bread, which is what that incomparable fragrance is that's floating around here just now."

I certainly am having the best *time,* Julia thought happily as she ran up after Dr. Penhallow, who was taking the steps easily three at a leap. Food — she'd never counted on that! On the upper floor quite different fragrances met her nostrils. Here there rose a sweet dried grass smell, like that in the Japanese shop, from straw matting laid along the broad floor of the airy hallway, a sandalwood fragrance seemed to come from the paneled walls, a camphor-wood smell from a large chest standing under a group of windows (Dr. Penhallow told her these last two when she asked, then a waft of lavender could be caught straying about in the air of a room they now entered.

And there was Kathryn Penhallow at last. She was sitting in a wheelchair, quite upright, looking fresh and just attended to, but very frail, with all the fire and energy of her being concentrated in eyes of so dark a brown as to seem almost black in the delicate face. Her pale red-gold hair was cut short. Her hands, quick as birds in their movements, Julia noticed later, were cupped together on a little table formed of a board attached by hinges to one arm of the wheelchair so that it could be lifted over across her lap to rest on the other arm. Here she could read or write or do whatever work she wanted on the pile of manuscripts lying within reach on her desk. She stretched out her hands to Julia who, warmed at once, came and took them.

"Sit down, child, over there on the couch where you can be comfortable and I can look at you and you can have a nice large tea on the coffee table." Dr. Penhallow went right to a big armchair which was no doubt his and explained to his wife that he had been so firmly expecting old Professor Goodall that he had looked down in absolute blankness at Julia. "Well," said Mrs. Penhallow, "I was expecting no one but Julia and I woke on the dot in time to be ready for her. My dear, I shall only be drinking a cup of tea, but I want you to eat heartily of all Mrs. Duncan's good food and pay no attention to me except to answer a question now and then."

In another moment here came Mrs. Duncan with a large tray covered with all that goes to make up a good, plentiful tea. I probably won't eat any dinner, Julia told herself fatefully, but it can't be helped. A person doesn't get food like this all the time, or hardly ever — and she accepted every single thing that was offered, and kept on being offered by Dr. Penhallow, until she couldn't hold another crumb and could only fill up the crevices with more cambric tea.

"Julia," said Kathryn Penhallow when everyone was settled with his cup of tea and plate of tarts and bread and butter and jam in front of him, "I must tell you at once that I feel your story to be a most remarkable one for a young person of your age to have written. Most remarkable! Most subtle and haunting!" Julia had stopped chewing in order to listen to these words of admiration in pure, respectful, absorbed silence, and then in a trance of joy continued to eat and taste and swallow. "Now I should like to ask you: was this story completely your own idea? It didn't, by chance, come from some grown-up conversation or idea? Not that that would have mattered, I suppose, as it was you who wrote the story. All the same, it would interest me to know whether or not the whole thing was entirely original with you."

Julia gazed at Mrs. Penhallow in anxiety. Here was that worrisome old question again: *was* the story really hers? And she told, then, of how it had been a dream, an incredibly clear and vivid and terrifying dream that had broken off at the point where she, and those she had come with, stood in front of the tall dark house and the door opened and there stood a man who took away his mask to reveal the face she had seen on the tapestry in the theatre.

"Then I made it up myself beyond the dream, from that place on. And it didn't seem any different to me but all a part of the whole story."

"And the important thing," Mrs. Penhallow took her up, "is that you were able to put both the dream-created part and the waking-created part into an organized whole in words and scenes that are real and absorbing to the reader. That is the test. Thousands of people tell formless bits of dreams — but what do they amount to? As for your story, I find myself dwelling on it, trying to work my way in to the heart of it."

"Only," said Julia, "I couldn't seem to make it finish the way a story should."

"Ah," said Dr. Penhallow, "but how *should* a story finish? Only in its own true way, surely."

"Perhaps, Julia," said Mrs. Penhallow thoughtfully, "perhaps you're not old enough yet to see to the bottom of your story. I think that it would take more experience than you can possibly have had to see how this extraordinary story should end, how it *must* end. And if you couldn't see farther, you were right to stop where you did. I must confess that the first time I read it through, I was disappointed. I wanted to be carried farther. I wanted some moment of complete understanding of the whole thing there at the end. But possibly this *is* the end and it's up to the reader to get his own understanding. Or maybe, someday, you will be able to tell us the true end and so, possibly, the meaning." Mrs. Penhallow held her cup of tea in both hands and gazed away as though listening to some future, distant Julia speaking that true end.

But Julia did not understand, or hoped she didn't.

"Then," she said, "you're not *going* to print my story now, not till I'm able to tell the true end and meaning of it?" It was the one outcome of this perfect experience she hadn't for a moment imagined. "But how can I ever tell? Why, I might be sixteen or seventeen by that time!"

Suddenly Dr. Penhallow put back his head as though about to burst into laughter, but bit his lip instead and exclaimed, "Dreadful! Dreadful!" And Mrs. Penhallow's face brimmed with delight that spilled over into a brilliance in her eyes which she directed straight at Julia.

"My dear, you won't be hopelessly aged by then. You'll still be able to get about and go on writing and send off your manuscripts. And it's true that I'm going to suggest that "The Mask" not be published in the *Gazette*. I've been thinking you should send it off to *St. Nicholas*. I can't be sure they'll take it, but you must try."

Julia put down her cup.

"That's where Leslie's poems are published."

"It is, and I think it high time you extended yourself beyond the Young Writers' Page in your hometown. You know the poet, Edna St. Vincent Millay, was first published in *St. Nicholas* and now she's famous and, so far, has four books of poetry. I keep thinking of Leslie — though who can tell about a girl of fourteen! But there's a gift both you and Leslie have, that any writer must have if he's to amount to anything, and that's the gift of seeing.

I so like the way you described the tall dark house in your story as looking to you, in the middle of the night, *warped.* That's excellent! You must always *see* clearly the objects you're describing, and find just exactly the right words to explain what you feel about the object, and how it looks."

"I will, Mrs. Penhallow," said Julia. "And I *do.* Especially before I go to sleep at night when I make stories come alive. Then I see everything down to the smallest detail."

Mrs. Penhallow studied her.

"Leslie called and told me about you —"

Julia's face lighted.

"She *did?* I thought someday — at least I wish that someday she would be my best — or at least," for a picture of Addie sitting at the dining table flashed into her mind, "one of my best friends."

A little later, when Dr. Penhallow got up and did not sit down again, Julia had a feeling that the visit had come to an end and that she should leave.

"I don't want you to go, Julia," said Mrs. Penhallow. "I have enjoyed this so much. But there are dozens of manuscripts I must go through — well, not must. Nobody is forcing me, except that I wouldn't disappoint any child and it makes me happy to think I may be encouraging some gifted one. Here is your story — as you'll see, I've made a few comments up and down the margins you might like to consider. Good luck, dear. Send it to *St. Nicholas.* I've put the editor's name and the address up there at the top."

Dr. Penhallow took the brown envelope for Julia, and on an impulse she went over to Mrs. Penhallow to clasp her hands again — but the hands came up and grasped her shoulders so that Julia leaned over and kissed her on her smooth, cool cheek and felt, as she did so, an intense spiritual energy flowing through those hands on her shoulders into her own self in a way she would never forget.

"Thank you — for the tea, and all you said —"

"I know — I know! And remember always to look, won't you? At the world, I mean. Soak it up — smell, listen, feel. *Look* at everything!"

"I will —"

Julia unreflectingly took the brown envelope and together she and Dr. Penhallow went out of the room and along the airy paneled hall with its grass matting and its huge, leafy windows, and down the wide stairs.

After dinner, Julia and Greg and their mother quite often sat at the table and talked in a relaxed way, feeling peacefully how the flurries of the day were over and saying things they didn't have a chance to say at other times. But usually it was Julia and her mother, because Greg liked to get into his reading in the brown leather chair that had been his father's, or he would go to his room to study. Tonight Greg was in the leather chair and Julia was still sitting at the table with her mother. She had reached over for her book, but she was not reading. She was staring straight out of the window in silence. She had already told them what had happened that afternoon at the Penhallows' and about how she had stopped by Leslie's to take "The Mask" to her.

But Leslie had not been there; she had forgotten. Yet Julia remembered distinctly Leslie saying, that Sunday afternoon down in the trees, "Come by here on your way home, why not?" Julia herself never forgot things that were important to her. Maybe Leslie didn't either. At any rate, she had left her story.

"What are you thinking, Julia?" her mother asked. "You seem so deep." Julia did not answer and her eyes dropped to the page of her book though she still did not take in the words. Her mother waited. "I do not see my children all day," she observed in that dry, self-mocking tone she sometimes used when she was making fun, "and when I come home and want a little companionship —"

"Quiet, please," said Greg, not looking up.

Julia grinned at her mother, who did not like to be disturbed in her reading any more than her children did. "I've been thinking about looking," she said. "That's what Mrs. Penhallow told me is important for a writer — looking at everything. *Seeing.* She said my word for the tall old house in my story, the way I saw it in the dark, was excellent. I said it looked warped." She felt her mother's hand on her arm.

"Look at me, Julia." And Julia turned. "Now close your eyes and describe the oak outside our window."

"It's big and gray," said Julia, who loved any game, "and the trunk is leaning toward the Parcels' house. And the limbs don't begin until high up, and they're very crooked and bending, and some have sharp elbows —"

"And what color are those high up — just now, I mean?"

"Well, gray, too. And the trunk and limbs are both rough —"

"Rough with little roughnesses?"

"Yes, little roughnesses. And the leaves are small."

"Is the trunk gray — pure gray?"

Julia, her eyes tightly closed, thought; tried her best to remember. "Yes," she said, puzzled. "Just gray."

"Well, look, then," said Mrs. Redfern.

And Julia looked. And the trunk wasn't pure gray. For over it there was a cast of the faintest, palest, pinkish orange, a wash of it up and down the whole huge, leaning bulk. And scattered over this faint wash of color were splotches of grayish-white, which Mrs. Redfern said were lichens. ("Oh, is *that* how you pronounce it!" said Julia, who had never thought of it as 'lie-kens.') And the limbs up there, at this moment, weren't gray, for in the sunset light far overhead they were the richest amber, a kind of rosy amber, and luminous on their undersides because of reflection from other limbs. The roughnesses on the trunk and limbs were not just small roughnesses, but large open splits as well as narrow cracks running lengthwise, some long, some short, some wavering. A grandfather oak it was, that may have been standing there for seventy-five years. Julia thought, as she looked, that she would probably never forget the least thing about this old trunk, nor the rosy amber limbs all bent and curving and elbowed there outside her mother's bedroom window.

"When I grow up to be a real writer," she said musingly, "I'm going to take care of you, Mother, and you won't ever have to worry about a thing."

"That's right," said Greg, considering. "We'll do that, Mom, even when you're old and messy and difficult."

"*Strangeness*," Julia wrote that night. "Mother gave me a piece of paper she'd copied something on because I like words. It says that an old woman told a friend that she found great support in that comfortable word Mesopotamia. And what is strange is that this is almost what I feel about Mediterranean. All I have to do is say to myself, the vast blue Mediterranean, and I get a feeling I don't know how to describe. I see this enormous sea all moving and trembling and glittering, the deepest blue you could ever imagine with light splintered across it, and I have a feeling of its being quaking and fathomless. Not the real Mediterranean, maybe — but *what* Mediterranean? And I say it over and over to myself because of what the saying does to me."

Chapter Ten

Julia was trying to write, to discover something, but it was hard. She was trying to get on with her story about the fantastical creature whose name had come to her in the middle of the arithmetic test — the harpet — but knew she would be balked in her efforts until she could minutely see it in her mind. What it did, she was beginning to understand, but its nature and appearance: that was a different matter entirely.

A week had passed since she had gone to the Penhallows' and it was now summer vacation. Pip Robinson, who lived directly behind the de Rizzios, had lately begun taking saxophone lessons and the pains of his practicing were being cast abroad for the entire neighborhood to share. "Tweedle, tweedle — squeal, squeal," he blew,

"tweedle, squeal, bloop — tootle, tootle — squeal, tweedle, bloop!" Now he gave up for a moment, possibly to
rest, then recommenced, as full of windy energy as ever.
Also, the Parcel children were contending together with
their usual vigor, and every word came up to Julia's room
even when she closed the doors and windows. Amidst out-
raged shouts a high-pitched howl arose.

"Mom-mm-eee! Taddy's hit me wiv a two-before —"
and the back screen door of the Parcel house slammed,
and the howls faded. A two-by-four was what little Hughie
meant, which is a particular thickness and breadth of a
piece of wood Julia knew. Mr. Parcel was a carpenter, and
his children were always hitting each other with special sizes
of wood.

"No, you can't play!" yelled Taddy to some other child.
"You're a girl and it has to be done *just right* —"

"But they're only mud pies —"

"Yes, but they have to be stirred a special way."

Along the street came the old rag and bottle man who
had been working the neighborhood thoroughly since
lunchtime. *"Hey,* whey'syuragsbolsacks?" he called in his
rough voice as though resentful of each door that remained closed. *"Hey,* whey'syuragsbolsacks?" over and over
and over again, in exactly the same tone, never varying by
so much as a second the intervals between the grating cries
that seemed wrenched out of his boots. His old horse
moved slowly, as along some rutted, desolate road out in
the country.

Now Greg appeared at the top of the stairs and flopped himself down beside Gretchy. He seemed aimless, discouraged, with all light and purpose gone out of him. Gretchy stretched herself into a scimitar, stretched until she trembled, yawned until you would have thought her jaws would come unhinged, then got up onto Greg's stomach and settled herself in a ball with her nose in her tail. He stroked her pensively.

"Watcha doing?"

"Trying to write a story about a harpet."

"What's a harpet?"

"I'm not sure yet —"

"Well, how can you write a story about a harpet if you don't know what a harpet is?"

Julia turned and gave him a look. "If I was just *let* to, maybe I could find out."

Greg considered this remark with interest, studying Julia as if turning over in his mind the idea of writing toward something or someone, gradually working one's way into the heart of a story until at last the mystery of it was revealed. "I'm stuck, too," he said finally, "on the eighth chapter of my history." His history of the Egyptians, he meant, and when Mrs. Redfern had asked him one day, when they had gone over to the museum in San Francisco and Greg was, as usual, not to be got out of the Egyptian Room, why he must labor so hard over his own history when there were already dozens, he turned and regarded her. "I don't see what that's got to do with anything," he said, and turned back to lean his elbows again on the glass above an especially fine mummy case, opened to reveal the emaciated bronze leather face and hands of some centuries-dead Egyptian, and then to look up as he thought — what? Sometimes, when Julia caught him looking away like that, she longed to ask, "Greg? Tell me —" because of his engrossed and wondering expression, as though he was lost in contemplation of some incredible sight. But it would be no use. What he knew, what he saw, he never felt like telling.

The almost unbelievable fact about Greg was this. On another occasion Uncle Phil had taken them to the Egyptian Museum in San Jose, and Mrs. Redfern, turning from a jewel case, let out a cry when she saw Greg standing under the elbow of the big statue of the Pharaoh Ikhnaton. She went to him and took off his glasses, leaving his face, Julia thought, naked and almost frighteningly unfamiliar. And when you looked back and forth at those two, you would have sworn that Greg and Ikhnaton were twin brothers. They stared at Greg's face, unusually narrow, with its full lips, slightly curved nose and almond-shaped, upslanting eyes, and then at the narrow face of Ikhnaton, with its full lips, curved nose and almond-shaped, up-slanting eyes gazing remotely into some long-gone Egyptian moment. Greg smiled at his mother.

"Yes," he said, "you see how it is."

"But, Greg, have you known?"

"For quite a while. I have a good face for an Egyptologist." He took his glasses, put them on again, and went away to an amulet case.

He might have been thinking of all this now, because he groaned suddenly, lying there with Gretchy on his stomach. "The twin brother of Ikhnaton — 1375 to 1358 B.C. — has to mow the front and back lawns and prune all those goldarned bushes! It's incongruous, that's what it is —"

"Yes, well, if you want to be an Egyptologist, you'd better hop along." Money was what Julia meant and the earning of it for his education, because their mother had nothing extra.

"You've got a nice room," said Greg peacefully. "It's much too light and open for my liking — positively made of windows. You might as well sleep in a park. But it's nice." At this moment the afternoon sun was not quite low enough to shine into Julia's western windows but was still sending a honey-colored shaft down the glassed-in light well so that the little room, with its white walls, was made to glow like the inside of a shell. The Parcel children had ceased their shouting, the old rag and bottle man had apparently worked his way over into some other neighborhood and all was still. Julia opened the balcony door and pulled back the three big casements over her desk and bed; the cool air flowed in, and the smell of grass and the sound of leaves.

"It's a perfect room," she said. She was looking down into the garden, having just spied Daddy Chandler heading for the woodshed and had determined what she was going to do next, for they had a series of little jokes going. "I wouldn't give it up for anything on earth." She said it with half her mind, but it was true. She had no need to think twice about it. She turned to Greg, smiling over her plan, and caught Greg slanting an odd look at her. He had been scratching Gretchy's face, under her chin, up around her ears, down her cheeks and then under her chin again, and she was in such an ecstasy that she lightly bit him then quickly licked the place and butted her nose into his hand for more delectable scratchings. But he put her gently aside and got off the bed.

"Not ever?" he asked. "Under any circumstances?"

"Oh, silly!" she said disgustedly. "Naturally, sometime — but that's centuries away." Then all at once, reflecting on that look of his, that odd, quick, questioning look, "What did you mean, Greg? Why did you look at me like that?"

But he was gone down the stairs and when he didn't answer, she knew it was no use teasing. Yet she thought of that look and saw it again in her mind's eye while she put her story away so that nobody should see it and try to read it in its embarrassing, half-finished state. Last Saturday she'd come up and found Kenny Kellerman here, sitting on her bed and pushing the cats around and pestering them, and he'd said Mrs. de Rizzio had let him in so that he could wait for her to come on out. But when had Ken ever wanted her to come out for any reason whatsoever, and Mrs. de Rizzio was astonished when she was told and said she had never done any such thing. Oh, he'd let himself in the back door, he confessed later, grinning. But *why* must he always lie the first time he was caught out in something he shouldn't have done? All the same, came into Julia's head as she locked her desk drawer, who hadn't lied at one time or another, and how many confessed the truth later as Ken had done, but just stuck to their lies no matter how knotted and twisted they became as the days went by?

When Julia arrived at the woodshed, she heard Greg up at the front of the house starting in on his mowing. The woodshed door was open and there in the sunlit, dust-moted interior was Daddy Chandler in his shirt sleeves. His shirt, as always, was immaculate and though he was about to do a job of physical labor, he had on his striped trousers, his stiff collar with the little wings in front, his black bow tie, and his derby hat which he wore for any expedition into the open air.

Now he picked up the hatchet, which he kept beautifully sharp, and began splitting a supply of kindling. And it was ridiculously easy, what with the noise of pine cracking and the gentle rubbing of a branch on the woodshed roof in the afternoon wind, to slowly close the door, lift over the latch, and slip the wooden peg down through its metal loop. No exclamation of surprise or of protest was heard. Julia ran around and peered through a dusty pane, but Daddy, always an intent old man, was completely absorbed in his work and seemed not in the least aware of the closed door, for there was plenty of westering sun flooding through the window on his right. Julia, bursting with glee, could not contain herself. She knocked on the glass and up came his eyes; he turned, saw the closed door, tried it, then sat down on the chopping block, shaking his head, rubbing a stiff old hand back and forth over his flyaway white hair and chuckling to himself. "By golly!" she heard him exclaim. "By golly, that Julia!"

"Got you, Daddy Chandler," she crowed, "got you! Now it'll be your turn —" She made a triumphant face at him, blew him a kiss, and ran off. In five minutes, or maybe in the time it would take him to get all his wood chopped, she'd be back to let him out. What a perfect joke, one she'd never thought of before. His last triumph had been to wrestle her off the rug in front of the Franklin stove in the de Rizzios' kitchen. The record, so far, had been an even one of wins and losses on both sides for all their jokes and competitions, but the other night Daddy had won two times in a row. And when Julia wanted another "go" Mrs. de Rizzio had intervened, standing there in her *Delsarte Speaker* position — her tiny feet in their pointed shoes in a precise V — with a bowl of potatoes in her hands and looking up at Julia, who was just slightly taller, with snapping blue eyes. No, no, she said. Julia sometimes forgot Daddy's age, which she must always remember. Daddy was far too old to be indulging himself in two wrestling matches one right after the other, let alone three, with a young whirlwind like Julia. She wouldn't have it, and besides dinner was ready.

"Far too old, rubbish!" said Daddy Chandler, his cheeks pink and his expression bright and lively. "I'm eighty-four."

"Daddy Chandler," shrieked Julia, hopping up and down, "you've *been* eighty-four for years. Mrs. de Rizzio says so."

Daddy let out a puff of laughter, straightened his tie, smoothed his hair, and went over to the table and began drinking his soup. "Exactly eighty-four," he said presently.

Well, he'd won that time, but now he was only one up. Julia was jogging along the drive to tell Greg, when here came Addie, shooting sparks of happiness and her hair bouncing.

"Paul's come, Julie," she shouted. "Paul's here —" and everything had turned out all right after all. She'd told her mother the other night how she and Julia had tried to make the living room look like the Redferns' and how Gram, in a fury, had ruined everything, and this morning Mom had gone right out and bought a lot of flowers and together they'd fixed it all just the way she and Julia had, only now the living room was even more beautiful, and Gram never said a word because Mom was so fired up. And when Paul and Aunt Kit and Uncle Norm had arrived, the front hall was cleaned up too and there were flowers on the table. And they'd been having more fun. Paul was quiet, but she still liked him as much as she had last time; in fact she liked him better than any boy she'd ever known. "Oh, and guess what, Julie, guess *what!* You know Aunt Kit and Uncle Norm are staying up at the Piedmont. Well, they've invited us up there for dinner, only Gram and Pop won't come — Mom says their noses are out of joint, whatever that means. Mad, I guess, be-

cause we're happy and talking and laughing and not paying them any mind. And just think, Julie, *I'm* going to eat
up at the Piedmont, too, just like you and Greg. I never
thought it would happen in this world. I can't believe it's
going to — can you? Is it going to, really?" Julia stood and
stared, unable to find a word to say. But already Addie was
oblivious. She grabbed Julia's hand and pulled. "We're
climbing on the new house up by our place, and Paul's
the best one. I told him about you —"

Away they went, and there was Paul, high up on the
rafters near the roof beams through which you could see
the sky. All the workmen had gone home and the house,
three stories, a tall, narrow, complicated mass of inter-
connecting beams, seemed to stand waiting in silent wel-
come for children to come and climb it, as if it had been
erected for that special purpose. Then here was Kenny at
her elbow, shoving his face close to hers, his gray eyes
madly alight with some wild excitation.

"Come on, fatty," he yelled. "Beat you to the top —"

"I'm *not* fat — I am *not* —!" Sturdy, her mother always
said she was, but not fat — she had never been that. Oh,
she hated Kenny for calling her fat with Paul up there.
She despised his lean little face with its jeering mouth and
squinting, mocking eyes, and his body, too small for his
age, and dirty, spider-like hands. In no time, because her
legs were longer than his, because she was just as quick,
and because she had seen at once which would be the fast-
est way, she had pulled ahead of him. Like a monkey, he
made his way over to her on an upward slant, got hold of

her ankle and began yanking, the first yank so unexpected that her fingers slipped, the skeleton house tilted and a flame of fear slit up through her stomach. Desperately she clung to a beam while Kenny got a good grip on her legs so that she was powerless to kick him off. And Addie, somewhere down below, joyously unaware, intent on her own climbing, laughed and kept calling out that she was going to beat them both and for Paul to watch her. "Paul — Paul — look, here I come — see, Paul — I can climb as good as you-u-u —"

"Ken, "said a voice, not very loud, but ominous, compelling. You heard the low warning right through Addie's high laughter and insistent cries. Kenny's arm loosened and instantly Julia kicked him off. He clung to a crossbeam, staring up at Paul, and when she could, Julia looked up too. "I just wanted to remind you, Ken," Paul said, and now he was just over them and she studied his brown face and short nose, his wide mouth that seemed, curiously, to be smiling in spite of the somber eyes that studied Kenny without blinking or wavering, "I just wanted to remind you that if you make somebody fall and they get killed, you're a murderer." He slipped down to stand beside Julia on the beam she was balanced on, and Kenny, crouched in a knot below, peered up at him. Julia, to her amazement, saw terror in Kenny's eyes.

"I am *not* a murderer — I am *not* — don't you go saying that, you goopy dope —"

"I'm not saying you *are* a murderer," replied Paul quietly, "I'm saying you could have been."

"I was just teasing her," shouted Ken frantically, as though Julia, even now, lay sprawled and still twenty feet below. "I didn't mean nothing. Don't you tattle — don't you tell my —" and then his thin lips closed and became almost invisible so that he looked like a little old man. And he turned and worked himself rapidly past Addie and on down.

"But what did he —?" asked Addie in bewilderment.

"Hello, Julia," said Paul, and he smiled at her.

"Hello," she said. But her face, in the shameful way it had, was turning red, and she was burning hot and still shaking from the awful vision of a shell of rafters whirling and tilting with space swaying open beneath her, and so she twisted round suddenly and began climbing again to test herself. But Paul put out his hand; he had hold of her skirt.

"Come on," he said. "Let's do something else."

"Yes, Julia, let's go play hide and seek," said Addie. "It'll be dark pretty soon, and that's when it's fun —"

"Me, too — me, too —" yelped Kenny down below, racing around in crazy circles, and then in one of those baffling changes of mood that so often swept him, "An' I tell you what, I'll be goal an' you all go an' hide."

He's trying to make us forget, thought Julia, swinging down. He's trying to get in good again. She jumped to the floor and as she ran past him saw how he squeezed up his face and grinned at her, then he leaned up against the house with his head on his arms, eyes hidden, and counted as loud and fast as he could. Addie was racing away. And now Paul had Julia by the arm and without so much as a glance at each other they ran around the new house to the back and then along between the Kellermans' yard and the one behind it.

"I know where to hide," she said. "Quick — it's across the street and Ken won't see us go. There's a big old windmill in back of that red house on the corner. It's Mrs. Moore's and she's away. No one will ever find us —"

Even as they pushed open the street gate of Rhiannon Moore's back garden, they heard Kenny yelling as he chased Addie toward "home." "Olly, olly, oxen free-e-e," she called, her voice ringing pure and clear all over the neighborhood. "Olly, olly, o-xen free-ee-ee —" The street-lights were coming on under the dusky blue dome of the sky, some in leafy caverns, others out in the open, and there, Julia noticed, as she glanced up at the globe above them, was that mysterious circle that leaves seem to make around whatever lighted lamp they are near. She led the way along the dark path to the mill door, and they forced it open and climbed the rickety stairs to a kind of broad shelf that had once been the upper floor where the machinery that turned the wind vanes could be greased. But the floor had fallen through twenty years ago, Rhiannon Moore had said, and the old wheel no longer turned, not even in the wildest wind, but only jerked and squeaked once in a while.

"How's this?" Julia made a clean place for herself among the cobwebs with a wad of old newspaper she had brought up another time for this very purpose. But she would not let herself, with Paul here, shudder over possible spiders. Paul dropped cross-legged and they leaned out of a little glassless window and surveyed with contentment the shadowed world beneath. The streetcar over on Grove ground by and its lights revolved on the mill's walls, then left them in darkness again. "My cats come up here," said Julia. "Now I know if I can't find them, this is where they might be. Once I came in and they both peeked over the edge of the floor, and then we all three stayed up here for about an hour. It's nice, with the trees thick all around. Nobody ever comes. I've never even told Addie about it because I'm scared she might let it out to Ken and then he and those big kids he goes around with might come up and find the cats. And then — you see, I can't trust him. They couldn't get past on these narrow steps — the cats couldn't — and it's too far for them to jump."

"But what would those kids want with your cats?"

"I don't know. Just meanness. Once I found them throwing stones at Sandy — just those other kids, not Ken — and they hurt his leg and I went for them and got a black eye."

Paul was silent, and she had an idea he was thinking about Ken. They heard Kenny and Addie shouting around the neighborhood for them, and they leaned together and laughed as if it were the most priceless joke in the world, and then Greg clanked the lawnmower over to the little tool shed at the side of the aviary. They watched the faint white blur of his shirt move over to the back door, he

banged in, then presently Julia's light went on and in surprised indignation she watched him across the garden as
he leaned over her desk, hunting for something. He found
it, seemed to be scribbling on a piece of paper, then
scrubbed out what he'd written and turned and went over
to the door.

"Eraser," said Paul. "Wanted to be sure it's the kind he
likes."

"Well, of all the *nerve*," exclaimed Julia. "My eraser!
Mother buys them at the five-and-ten, but Greg can never
find his in all that junk he keeps in his room. He probably
eats them."

They sat in silent companionship, listening to the sounds
of evening. Julia wanted this time never to end, but
thought guiltily of how she should be indoors, setting the
table for dinner and putting two saucepans of water on to
boil and peeling the potatoes. "When I was six or seven,"
she said, "Mother took me to a picture show, and it was
about two nuns who were locked up in a tower by their
enemies — high up, where no one could ever hear them.
There were little slits in the tower way over their heads,
so all they could see was the sky, but they heard an army
down below, marching past, and the army was singing
'Onward Christian Soldiers' — you know":

On-ward Chris-tian so-o-o-ldiers, [sang Julia]
Marching as to-o war,
With the cross of Je-e-sus
Going on before.

Christ, the royal ma-a-ster [Paul joined in]
Leads against the foe.
Forward into ba-a-ttle.
See His banners go.
On-ward Chris-tian so-o-o-ldiers, [stern and magnificent]
Marching as to-o war,
With the cross of Je-e-sus
Go-ing on be-fore!

They were silent for a moment after they'd finished, savoring to the full the deep satisfaction of having sung in unison, without a single mistake or a stumble, a whole verse and the chorus. Then, "And they starved to death up there," went on Julia, "and years and years later some people broke the door open and there were their bones, lying in a heap of dust and old rotted cloth. Oh, I cried and cried because I'd never seen anything so sad in my life. Just imagine being up there like that, without anything to eat, and not being able to make anyone —" Suddenly Julia's breath caught and her hands flew to her mouth. She leaped up. "Oh, Daddy — Daddy Chandler!" and with horribly shaking legs that had no strength in them, that would scarcely hold her, she somehow got down that black, steep flight, pushed and hauled her way past the warped door that always stuck on its sill, tore past bushes that impeded her and scratched her face, yanked open the gate into the de Rizzios' garden, and raced along the path toward the back hedge.

"Daddy," she shouted, "Daddy — I'm coming — I'm coming —"

To her utter astonishment she saw light streaming through the little windows of the woodshed. She pressed her face to one of them and there was Daddy, still sitting on the chopping block, which he had pushed back so that he could lean against the wall, and he had a big book on his knees which he was peacefully reading by the light of an oil lamp that sat on the shelf above his head. He had taken off his derby hat, and he looked like an old prophet in the flood of soft orange-yellow pouring over him in a pool in the midst of peaked shadows. He had cut a pile of kindling and split some logs into the sizes his daughter liked for the fireplace, and these he had stacked neatly according to thicknesses under the shelves of magazines and discarded books.

With clumsy fingers, Julia got the peg out of its metal loop, pulled open the door, knelt beside the old man with her arms around him and pressed her face against his arm. She could not have told what awful thing she expected might have happened to Daddy because she had forgotten him, but she began to cry with relief. And then, how strange — for Daddy Chandler was shaking, and when she lifted her face she saw that he was laughing. And he laughed and laughed in absolute silence as he gazed down at her, and then his hand came up and rested on her head. Finally he gave a gasp, got out his big white handkerchief, and wiped his papery lids edged with their sparse lashes. "Oh, my!" he said. "I declare, I declare! Now we're even, aren't we, Julia? Or just about, by Jasper. But you wait," he said, uncontrollable bursts of amusement still escaping him. "I've had a chance to do some thinking, locked up in here. You just wait —" and he got the little bag of peppermints out of his trouser pocket and offered her one.

Chapter Eleven

Julia stood on a promontory of rock high in the Berkeley hills not far from the Grizzly Peak fire lookout. She could hear Addie and Ken shouting up in the pine grove somewhere, careering around like puppies let out of a pound, and Dr. Carlson's voice ringing occasionally as he called some warning to them about poison oak. Paul shouted once, but the voices of neither Greg nor Leslie, who were walking together, were to be heard. Dr. Carlson was talking steadily to Daddy Chandler, and Daddy was of course just quietly listening as he always listened to Julia chattering away when they came up alone.

The two of them had started out after lunch together for their usual walk in the hills, and Greg, for some reason, decided he wanted to go too. And when they had passed the Kellermans', there were Addie and Paul and Ken just back from somewhere with Paul's mother and father. And when the six of them got up near the hills, Julia thought of Leslie's house just along the street, and when she ran up the steps to ask if Leslie had finished the story and if she would like to come, Dr. Carlson answered the door and said he was sick of sticking at his desk. He hadn't been for a hike up there for years — it was just what he needed, to get away from his eternal scribbling in the margins of papers. Leslie told Julia at once that she thought "The Mask" must be sent off to *St. Nicholas* and that she would give it to her when they got back.

The promontory where Julia now stood was her favorite place of any she and Daddy had discovered, and she had left the others a moment before to run out here and look over all of Berkeley and Richmond and the bay and San Francisco and Marin County. It was an enormously wider, more splendid view than any to be had from down there where the last houses thinned out into wooded slopes around the rock quarry. Immediately beneath her a vast stretch of tall golden grasses — the wild oats — waved on the steeply sloping breast of this upland meadow, dried in the summer sun, bending where the wind laid an invisible hand, then rising again when the wind lifted and wandered on. And the grasses were strewn so thickly with poppies that in places the hillside seemed running with drifts of orange fire. Behind her stood an enclosing amphitheater of pines and from one of the pines a white-crowned sparrow sang, "Swee, swee, sweeee-eee, swee-

swee," and blackbirds sent forth their liquid burblings and whistlings. No one had noticed her when she ran off ahead. Only a hawk, gliding in spirals high in the blinding blue, held her in his tiny eye as he swept over the hills. A squirrel chattered at her for invading his privacy, and a crow answered the squirrel, then sailed off right over her head and she heard the whuff-whuff-whuff of his wings winnowing the air.

She stood looking out, then suddenly, bethinking her of a kingdom, she lifted her arms and held them with her hands extended, palms down, as if conferring a blessing.

"These lands are mine," she intoned. "I pronounce them mine." Here she made sweeping gestures of possession, which, to anyone who might have been observing her from a distance, would have seemed to indicate that she was doing some form of exercise, or warding off especially pesty insects, or possibly that she was touched in the head. "And that part yonder," she went on, "to the left beyond the white spire of my castle" (she meant the campanile on the university grounds) "shall from thence and forward be known as Atlandia, and the land on my middle left as Palgravia, and there in front of this place whereon I stand as Norondia, and that yonder to my middle right as Nostromulus, and there to my far right, as far as eye can behold and discern, as Hereldon. And now these, my lands, have been named, and shall be called by these names from this day forth, and my various and wideflung peoples as — as —" (here Julia stood motionless for a moment with her arms still extended while she tried to

remember) "oh, yes — as Atlandians and Hereldians —
I mean, Hereldons — no, I like Hereldians better. Cross
out Hereldons," she ordered the scribe who sat at her feet
with a roll of parchment crackling out over his lap, "and
put Hereldians. I trust you know how to spell it," she said
severely at the top of his bald head. "And also Nostrul-
muns." But that wasn't right. "No, Nostromuluns — and,
golly, I've forgotten some. Anyway, put down that they're
all — I mean that the people of every separate land shall
be gathered together from now unto all time as one people
under the single name of my vast and united kingdom,
Himalterranea. So be it. I, the Queen of Himalterranea,
has spoken — I mean, *have* spoken." She cast a stern eye
upon her ministers to see that none was snickering at her
mistake. But to a man, one minister for each land, and
clad in sumptuous robes (but not nearly so sumptuous as
her own), they were bowing and murmuring assent, gathered together in a little group. It is true that they were
only a heap of rocks and that their voices were pine boughs
brushed by the wind, but the sound was assuredly like the
hushing of assent, "Yess-s-s, your Highness-s-s — yess-s,
your Highness-s-s-s!" She listened contentedly, swept a
last glance over her kingdom, then turned and ran back
through the trees to where everybody was going on down
around a bend in the path. "Chooloop, chooleep, chooloop, chooloop, chooleep, chooloop," she sang to herself
as she ran. She'd have to ask Mrs. Moore what kind of
bird *that* was. But she could never hope to imitate those
clear, pure notes.

Greg was still telling Paul and Leslie about his history of the Egyptians. Leslie, her eyes going from pines to sky to distant prospect of bay and ocean and mountains, said nothing but only laughed that sudden infectious laugh of hers now and then that seemed always to make Paul say something which he plainly hoped would be funny, and sometimes Leslie thought it was. Dr. Carlson was still lecturing Daddy Chandler on early California. Addie was skipping along beside Paul, and Kenny was a little way ahead trying to climb the side of a rock as big as a cabin and shouting out bulletins at intervals on what progress he was making.

Julia came along behind Paul and Addie and put her arms through theirs and pulled them aside. "There's a house over there," she said, pointing, "a little place that an old man used to live in when Daddy and I first began coming up here, and Daddy and he used to talk while I explored. But the last time we came, he was gone, and the door was all boarded up, and the windows. But when we looked in between the boards, everything was just the way he'd left it — the dishes on the table, and his clothes on the bed, and the bedclothes, and the pots and pans on the stove, and newspapers lying around where he'd dropped them and everything was dusty. Daddy Chandler said maybe his family came and got him and didn't think anything of his was worth taking away."

When they drew near, they saw that it would be no use going up to the windows to view the mysterious scene Julia had described, for the boards had been wrenched from the windows, the panes were broken, and the door stood ajar, hanging from a single hinge. Nothing would be left inside but wreckage. Tramps, no doubt, said Dr. Carlson, or boys just as likely. Julia ran over to be certain, and as she came within a short distance of the house she saw a gray rabbit resting on its front feet with its belly on the ground and just ready, apparently, to pull its hind legs through a narrow, jagged opening between the wall and the floor. "Hullo, rabbit," she said, stopping. But it did not move, only watched her with bulging, terrified eyes, its ears straight up. Why, it looked exactly like Peter Rabbit crawling under Mr. McGregor's gate, she thought, only it hadn't a blue jacket on. Suddenly it gave a convulsive movement but, to her astonishment, it did not run. Her stomach gave a strange little prick and as she came nearer, she understood. It was caught. Its hind legs were caught in that jagged rent in the wood, and it could not get free. She heard the rest of them coming behind her; she heard Kenny yelling, "Hey, looky there — a rabbit, a rabbit — oh, *boy*, it's caught! Just looky there — I claim it — it's mine — I saw it before anybody —" and he was abreast of her and about to lunge for the rabbit when all at once it screamed.

It stared up at the enormous shapes closing in on it, and it opened its mouth and a loud, clear, piercing cry of anguish tore through the pink gullet. Julia flung her arms around Kenny and held on fiercely as they toppled and rolled, and Leslie's father reached down and gripped him and Kenny writhed and scratched and beat at Dr. Carlson's restraining hands and kicked at his legs in a wild fury.

"It's mine — I saw it first —" He was, himself, like a little passionate, snarling animal being kept from its prey.

Julia went slowly over to the rabbit and it screamed again and struggled madly, and she got her hand through an opening in the boards just above it and felt the dead cold pads of its hind feet. Gently, in horror of its pain, she tried to work the hind legs free while resting her other hand on its head in the hope of soothing it. But suddenly she was shoved to one side.

"If that rabbit bites you," said Paul, "you'll be poisoned. There's a rabbit virus —" He got the toe of his shoe under the rotten board nearest the floor, forced it up until it cracked, and the rabbit tried desperately to drag itself away but seemed unable to move. Paul took off his sweater and wrapped it around the frantic thing, then took it into the underbrush. Kenny was yelling and struggling.

"Ken," said Leslie, "what are you making such a fuss about? Why shouldn't the rabbit be free?"

"I want it — it's mine. I just want it. I'll make a cage."

"Not now you won't," she said with deep, calm satisfaction.

But like a little quick fish he'd slipped from Dr. Carlson's grasp and was racing over to where Paul had disappeared. And then Paul came out of the trees and met Kenny head on. Paul smiled at him and put out an arm and closed his fingers around the back of Kenny's neck.

"It's gone," he said lightly, as if indifferent. "It hopped into a hole down under the bank. You'd never find it. Did you know that a rabbit's hole is called its form?"

"What'd you do that for?" demanded Kenny, his little face scarlet with rage. "What'd you let it go for? I wanted it — you didn't have to let it go —" Paul let his arm drop and Kenny went rooting into the underbrush among dark brownish-red branches of madrone and manzanita and through clumps of wild sage. Julia glanced up from where the scuffling was going on and saw Paul turn and look at them as though to say, "Don't worry — he won't find it." And she was aware, as she had been the first time she saw him, of the wry, not quite hidden humor of his mouth and eyes, even when his face was grave. Then Kenny crawled out, his blond hair standing up in foolish little peaks and stuck with leaves and bits of twigs.

"I think, Ken," said Dr. Carlson, "that a wild rabbit would die in a cage."

"It would," said Paul. "That's exactly what would happen."

But Kenny never looked at them. Silently, head lowered, he trotted off down the hill, going fast, never glancing back, and presently was out of sight.

"Mom doesn't know what to do with him," observed Addie in an elderly tone.

"Is he always like this, child, so desperate about everything?" asked Dr. Carlson.

"Oh, yes — well, that is, not always. But if my father's been at him and whaling him for something he is. And then, sometimes, for several days he'll be all right and you'd never think he could be so ornery and impossible. Of course, my father —" But suddenly Addie didn't seem to care to go on. Her eyebrows went up, she shrugged and turned away. "It's nice up here. I've never been this high up, not to the lookout. I hope the rabbit's all right. Will it be, Paul? Did it really go into its — whatever a rabbit's home is?"

"No," said Paul. "I just put it down in a dark place between two rocks and pulled branches over. I knew Kenny wouldn't notice, and he didn't. He never went near the rabbit, but it won't be able to move for a while."

"Its legs," said Greg, "being caught like that, and paralyzed because the blood was cut off. But it'll flow back."

"Was that why —" Julia began, then knew she dare not finish. And it was because of the rabbit's scream, which had been one of the shocks of her life: the note in that high, terrible, almost human cry of desperate finality, so that the hairs had risen on the back of her neck and down her arms, and the skin on them had gone tight with gooseflesh. It was because of the feel of its pads, as though they were dead, the blood on her hand from its scraped legs, the fury of Kenny's determination and not knowing what designs he had had on the rabbit, what cruelty he might be capable of. She swallowed so as to get the better of herself. "Was that why its feet were so cold — like ice?" Her voice shook.

"Yes, that was why," Leslie said. "But it's safe now, Julia."

"But if we hadn't *come*," she persisted, "if I hadn't *seen* it, what would have happened? What if Kenny had come up here with those boys he knows —"

"Jule," broke in Greg, flat and impatient, "you're at it again. 'What if — what if — what if —?' You go on and on like that, and it's no use. You stay awake all night wondering 'what if?'. The rabbit's all right. We *did* come. We *did* see it. And Ken's gone home."

"But why did it scream?"

"Because," said Paul, "it thought it was finished. Rabbits hardly ever make a sound, but if a rabbit is surrounded and sees no way out, it will scream."

If she could have gone off by herself into the woods and sent up a great wail, it would have been the most enormous relief, but she walked with her head turned away and her throat on fire and once when she looked round she saw Daddy Chandler watching her, and he smiled and gave her a little nod of encouragement.

By the time they got down to the Carlsons', he was tired. He looked out of puff, Dr. Carlson said, and he must come in and have a rest and Leslie would make him some hot tea. Though he protested that, considering his age, he was in pretty good shape, he did go in and consented to being settled on the lounge with a pillow behind his back. Leslie went into the kitchen to put the kettle on and make lemonade for the rest of them, while Dr. Carlson went from chair to chair picking up mending here and knitting there and darning from the couch, all of which he bundled together and threw into a corner. The living room, with its row of windows on the view side, was a long, rather bare place, done up in chintz that was faded to a nondescript blur and grown soiled and shiny on the chair and sofa arms. None of the coverings fit very well and all of the projects going on seemed half finished, like the mending and knitting and darning, as well as books lying about with slips of paper stuck in halfway through and piled up on whatever surface was available. The fireplace was filled with tossed in papers.

"Sorry for the mess," Dr. Carlson said to Daddy Chandler, and swept aside an accumulation of opened mail on the coffee table to make room for Leslie's tray of lemonade. But it was plain the mess bothered him no more than it bothered Daddy, or Greg, who was already lost in the book he'd found on the floor beside his chair. Addie, subdued, sat politely nearby, her legs swinging, and Paul stood looking out of the windows at Uncle Phil's new house and down at the eucalyptus grove where, Julia told him, she'd met Leslie. Presently Leslie came in with the tea, poured cups for Daddy Chandler and her father, and handed round the lemonade and some rather dry but not quite inedible raisin cake. Then she went out, her shoes clattering along the hardwood floors scattered rather sparsely with throw rugs, and Julia heard her run upstairs. When she came back she had Julia's story and the June *St. Nicholas,* which she handed Julia with a little smile and Julia, without needing to ask, turned to the back of the magazine.

Yes, there it was — a new poem by Leslie. It was called, simply, "Hymn."

> *When I was a child, leaning against my mother,*
> *Drowsing through the droned Word of God,*
> *I woke to the organ's jubilation*
> *With heart swelled big as an anthem,*
> *Beating like a bell,*
> *Though why I could not tell*
> *When we stood up to sing*
> *Holy, holy, holy,*
> *Lord God Almighty,*
> *And I could have risen like the cherubim*
> *Through spheres of sunny space,*
> *Pealing my praise*
> *In joyous innocence.*

Julia read it over again. But it was far too short! She wanted it to go on, she wanted to know more about that child, the long-ago Leslie, who had sat in some high-vaulted church with the light pouring down on the congregation in slanting golden planes and feeling the almost uncontainable rise of emotion when the organ boomed and reverberated. She did not know what to say and, without looking at Leslie, touched Greg's arm and handed the magazine to him and pointed, then sat there watching him and sipping her lemonade and finishing her cake.

He slapped the magazine down on his knees and stared at Leslie, who sat opposite him on the floor with her knees drawn up and her skirt pulled over in a tent with her arms locked round and her chin resting on them. For a little he studied her without saying anything and she met his eyes steadily with no embarrassment.

"That is exactly," he said presently, "what I felt when I was a little kid and my grandmother took me to church. I mean this was *exactly* it — and we used to sing 'Holy, Holy, Holy,' and I liked that hymn better than any other. I'd go off to sleep during the sermon, and then the organ would begin, and this hymn. Just the way you have it here was the way it was and the way I felt."

"That's what a poem is," Leslie said, "a feeling about some special time or place or happening, pressed into as few lines as it will go."

That night Julia wrote, "We all came together like streams running into a river, first Daddy and Greg and me, then Paul and Addie and Ken, then Dr. Carlson and Leslie. And now Leslie is my true friend, not instead of Addie but added to Addie. And I wish we could all go on forever and be friends always, except for Ken, and that Paul would stay. Next week we're going to have a party for Greg's birthday. Mother asked him if he'd rather invite his own friends, but he doesn't have many because he's always coming home and shutting himself in his room. The boys he knows at school he just sees there and hardly ever asks them here. And he said he likes Paul and Leslie and wants them to come, but we don't know what to do about Ken. We have to ask him and I wish we didn't." Julia paused to think, and then, "I can't write anything about the rabbit, but I will never forget it. I hope I don't dream about it, though even if I don't dream, I'll see the whole thing all over again as if it was happening, and it will be real, not just remembering. I'll keep rescuing the rabbit over and over, only nobody will be there but Ken and maybe those others he goes with. I wish I wouldn't do this. You'd think if I rescued an animal once that would be enough, but it's as if I have to be *sure*. I try to make myself stop, but I can't and the seeing goes on and on."

Chapter Twelve

Julia hauled up the bedclothes and plumped herself down on the wrinkles and humps with Mr. Yeats's big book of poems on her knees and her toes pointed in. She turned over the pages, muttering to herself as she read, deciding what slips of paper to leave. When Mrs. Moore got home, she would have to admit to her that she had really liked and understood perhaps only four or five of all the poems marked, but those, at least, very much, and she wanted to be able to show her which ones.

She slapped the book shut and stretched out a hand to the pen and pencil holder where the key to the red house had been kept since Mrs. Moore left, then frowned in puzzlement. It wasn't there. She pulled out the string she wore around her neck to discover if, in some lost and unconscious moment, she might have unknotted it and slipped on Mrs. Moore's key. But only the usual three lay on her palm, one for the desk drawers, one for her own front door, and one for her skates. When you skate downhill, she remembered distractedly, your skates go per-clocketa, per-clocketa, per-clocketa over the lines in the pavement if the hills are only slightly sloping, but nick-nick-nick-nick-nick when you skim down in a swoop on the steep ones — a discovery she'd made yesterday coming home from Leslie's. *But where was Mrs. Moore's key?* So it usually was: foolish, random thoughts mixed up in her head even when she was most scared about something.

She turned over the pen and pencil holder, a handsome, heavy china one, pale blue green, with "A remembrance from Janssen Piano Co. 1924" printed on the bottom, that her mother had brought home from the music store for one of her desk appurtenances (that was Greg's word). Pins, rubber bands, small keys to forgotten keyholes, an expired moth, an old dusty fly as well as pens and pencils dropped onto the blotter. But no big door key. In a panic Julia pawed through the side drawers then unlocked the center one and dumped it upside down on the floor.

"Greg — *Greg* — have you got Mrs. Moore's key? I can't *find* it!" She leaped downstairs two at a time, and pushed open his door and there he sat, cross-legged, in the midst of what appeared to be a heap of rubble. Certainly there were rocks among it, bits of iron, unrecognizable oddments of wood, innumerable frayed notebooks and a litter of old newspapers and magazines. This morning

173

his mother had said, before leaving for her Saturday half-day at work, that his room *must* be cleaned — tomorrow, if he liked, though if he wanted to show Leslie and Paul his Egyptian art, it might be an idea to straighten it up today and open the windows and let out the stuffy smell. She had uttered the words "straighten up" in the most ironical tones, for you had only to glimpse the chaos that surrounded Greg in his private haunt to realize that straightening would be but the simplest beginning, a mere idle ruffling of the surface.

"On my *birthday?*" he had cried in pure horror.

Nevertheless, there he sat. He gazed up at Julia wearily, with complete disinterest, then apparently decided to take pity on her. Sighing, he rested his elbows on the points of his knees and clasped his hands.

"When you last went into Mrs. Moore's house to water the plants, you undoubtedly did one of two things," he began patiently in his best Sherlock Holmesian manner. "Either you left the key in the lock and it's still sitting there — at least hopefully, if some sly peddler hasn't spied it, snitched it, and then driven up in a van and made off with every last thing in the place — *or,* you laid the key down somewhere inside, did the watering, then came out and of course allowed the door to lock behind you as it is supposed to do. So that, as you cannot now go back, all the plants will slo-o-wly shrivel, which depressing sight will be the first to meet Mrs. M's horrified eye upon her weary arrival home. And this will undoubtedly take place at some bleak and chilly hour when all she wants is a hot bath and the reassurance that you, Julia Redfern, have been faithfully fulfilling that facile promise you made when she so naively entrusted her affairs to you. Now kindly close *my* door behind you, child, and I will get on with this evil task."

Shattered, Julia left at once and ran out across the grass, down the gravel drive, around onto Mrs. Moore's lawn and up the front steps. There was no key in the door. Taken? By that sly peddler? She tried the door; it was locked. And then she could have wept with joy, for all at once she knew as clearly as if she were actually watching herself do it, that she *had* taken the key inside and laid it down somewhere while she trotted back and forth with pitchers of water. And somehow Greg and Mr. de Rizzio would be able to get in for her so that she could go on keeping her promise to Mrs. Moore about the plants.

She went back along the drive humming to herself and heard the phone ring as she banged the screen door.

"Julia?" inquired Leslie's voice. "Yes, it's me. What am I going to get Greg?"

"Wait a minute —" Julia peered into the hall to be sure Greg's door was still closed and it was, and he could not possibly have heard anything considering the violence of scraping and shuffling going on behind it. "I think he must be moving all his furniture, which means he's gone insane — and on his birthday, too! Anything Egyptian, Leslie. *Any*thing, doesn't matter what."

"Does he have whole shelves full of books on Egypt?"

"Well, no, not exactly. He has a sort of tome that Uncle Phil gave him last year, and then quite a few thin ones he's found in secondhand bookstores —"

"Anything beautiful?"

"*Beautiful!* I should say not! They all look boring and ugly — little tiny print and rows and rows of hieroglyphs and diagrams of tombs and stuff like that."

"Good —"

Leslie came to the party at fifteen minutes past the appointed hour, which was six, with her hair done up and earrings swinging at her ears. She looked at least seventeen, and something happened inside Julia the instant she saw her. Later, in bed that night when she went over everything as she always, afterwards, did go over momentous happenings, she knew that it was because she thought she had lost Leslie.

Ken hadn't come and was not coming. He wanted to stay at home and be left alone, Addie reported. Besides, parties, he said, gave him a pain. She and Paul arrived early and lighthearted, each bearing a package. Now they all turned and watched Leslie walk across the grass, and when she drew near, Greg, with an exclamation, went to her, crossed his arms on his chest and lankily leaned over to have a good stare at the earrings.

Leslie turned her head with dignity to look at him.

"Scarab beetles in drops of amber," she said. "They were Grandmother's. Granddad gave me them when she died, and this one on a gold chain." She lifted it from her neck. "I don't wear the earrings much because Dad says they're too old for me. I ought to give them to you, Greg, except that they're heirlooms."

"Well, I wouldn't take them," he said indignantly, his eyes riveted.

"But they should be yours. The little metal parts could come off. Do you like my hair up?" she asked unexpectedly of Julia and Addie, and in the fresh, unthinking directness of that question, tossed away in a moment the three years Julia had unhappily added to her age.

Mrs. Redfern came out with a big bowl covered with wax paper and put it down on one of the two card tables standing side by side and set for dinner. "So this is Leslie," she said. "I heard the question and I think your hair is elegant."

But Greg shoved his hands in his pockets and turned away. "Well, *I* think you look like somebody's aunt," he said. Whereupon Leslie reached up, plucked out some pins and a clasp, and the whole shining mass fell halfway down her back.

Julia said they must all go in and see Greg's Egyptian art, otherwise he would have killed himself cleaning his room for nothing. Displayed on his walls were three large maps of Egypt at different stages in its history, all in clear, vivid watercolors on thick white paper and decorated with drawings of the Egyptian gods in firm outlines in jet black ink: the Apis bull and Bast the cat, Horus the hawk, Anubis the jackal, Thoth the ibis. There was a frieze of figures standing in their curious twisted postures along the tops and bottoms of the maps. All details, and the precise lettering, Greg had obviously drawn with absorbed devotion. There were paintings of the pyramids with a diagram in the corner of each showing the interior, and there was a quite remarkable life-size painting of Ikhnaton. Julia made Greg take off his glasses and stand beside it.

"My sacred ancestor," he announced, "portrayed by a respectful descendant."

There was a little silence.

"Are you really?" asked Addie in a faint voice. "You couldn't be!"

"Do you mean that *that*," exclaimed Paul, "is exactly the way this pharaoh looked?"

"Exactly the way," said Greg.

Addie put her hands to her mouth. "It's spooky!" she cried. "The Egyptians were a million years ago. You give me the creeps, Greg."

"Not me," Paul said. "Because when you see the painting, and then Greg, you know everything isn't just ordinary after all. I mean, there really are mysteries."

"Strangenesses," said Julia. "Of *course!*" Some days there were so many she couldn't put them all down, yet here was Paul, who lived in Canada and who'd gone camping in the Canadian Rockies where there were glaciers that had been lying in the clefts of peaks for maybe a thousand years, he had told them, and who'd seen with his own eyes bear and elk and moose and mountain lions, saying maybe everything wasn't ordinary after all, just as if he thought everything was. And here she had envied him!

Leslie stood silent, intently studying the painting and then Greg's face, and when finally he put his glasses on again, Julia thought: now she'll make a poem about it because it's magic to have happened after all these centuries here in this country when we're English and Irish and Scotch. And when Mrs. Redfern came in and told them how she had imagined Greg in the future, a professorish sort of bachelor surrounded by his "stuff" that would close in on him as the years went by — a mass of possessions, she teased him, instead of a family —

"Oh, I don't know," Leslie said with a certain lightness and a lift of the eyebrow.

She had given him a book of Egyptian tomb paintings, it was discovered when he opened his presents, and Greg, who usually had no difficulty finding words, said nothing, only sat there turning over the richly colored plates and then went back to the flyleaf. "For Greg," Julia read over his shoulder, "on his fifteenth birthday, from Dr. and Mrs. Newman Carlson and Leslie."

"But, Leslie," said Mrs. Redfern, "it's far, far too —"

"No, it's not," she said quickly. She was watching Greg's face. "My father's always been interested in anyone who knows so young — I mean, the way Greg does — what he's going to do. And we've had the book for a long time. It's from all of us because I'd have inherited it some day."

"Now my library," Greg said with solemnity, "has really begun. And any foul creature caught laying its grubby paws on these pages shall be instantly *withered.*"

Paul had found a tie, dark blue with a green "kind of hieroglyph design," he thought it was, and Addie an owl tiepin because she was sure the Egyptians had liked owls. "Didn't they, Greg?" He turned over the leaves of Leslie's book and there, sure enough, was a handsome though rather weary-looking owl (possibly, Greg said, he had been up too late reveling, to judge from the circles under his eyes, and there was, certainly, a wine jug standing by his claws). It was a detail from a painting in the tomb of Seti I, XIX Dynasty, 1303–1290 B.C. "I knew it!" exulted Addie. "I had a feeling!"

Julia, when she and her mother had gone to the museum in San Francisco to get their gifts, had chosen the figure of a sitting cat about four inches high, duplicated in metal from an Egyptian tomb piece and mounted on a heavy base so that it could be used as a paperweight. It had long legs, large upstanding ears, a locket around its neck, and a bright, knowing expression. "I was *especially* taken with its expression," Julia told Greg. "Golly, Jule, I'll bet it took every penny you had —" "Oh, it did," said Julia with deep satisfaction, "and a little bit more besides. But it was worth it." Greg obviously thought so too. "I'll use it on my desk until I die."

And then Greg lifted over the heavy, oblong box that had a tag, "From Mother and Uncle Phil." And when it was opened and the top excelsior pulled aside, there lay a replica of the head of Queen Nefertiti, the face serene, the full lips not quite smiling, the large tilted eyes gazing into a private world which appeared to afford her eternal pleasure. "She was one of the most beautiful women who ever lived," Julia told Addie and Paul. "Greg's always wanted an Egyptian statue, and this is the only largish one they had over at the museum." Again Greg seemed, for a moment, unable to say anything. He held the head and smoothed a hand over it. "I'm going to make a special stand for her. And clear a place — a special place." He seemed to picture the scene. "And maybe even keep it cleared," he added seriously.

Dusk changed to dark while they sat at the card tables eating supper. Julia and Greg had put candles inside the paper lanterns Mrs. Redfern had bought at the Japanese shop around the corner from the music store, and had strung them from limbs the old oak held out above the aviary and over the grass. Their mellow light made a pool in which the card tables seemed to float. Or it was as if they were all laughing and joking and eating fried chicken and bean salad and hot buttered rolls inside a large golden balloon through whose top you could look up and see the thousand stars scattered across the night sky. Scent of roses, of broom and damp grass and earth and crushed eucalyptus cups drifted together. Julia thought how, in the light of the lanterns and the candles on the tables, they all looked different from their everyday selves, more alive, more exciting, their glittering eyes going constantly from face to face. They were laughing at something Leslie had said, though she herself only smiled. And it seemed as if she was the center, as if it were her party. You couldn't have explained why, but it would never matter that Leslie wasn't beautiful — was, in fact, almost plain. She would always be the center.

Julia, whose back was to the aviary where the canaries occasionally let out surprised, questioning cheeps, happened to glance up at the dark block of Mrs. Moore's house rising behind the eucalyptus trees — then put out a hand on Addie's arm on one side, and on Paul's on the other.

"Look!" she said. "Up there —"

In the midst of laughter they all, oddly enough, heard what she said and turned. A small gleam, that rose and sank and rose again, hovered in the darkness of the rear upstairs window, the one above the driveway. Then it moved, disappeared, and was next to be seen at one of the windows above the back garden. From there it went to the window beyond, and then to the one beyond that, as though somebody holding a candle were searching for something in Mrs. Moore's bedroom. Now the faint radiance moved away and after several moments of continued absence someone commenced to play the piano. After which the candlelight, or whatever light it was, reappeared at the back window while the one who played continued.

"But — I don't understand," said Julia in a shaken voice, "because that's Mrs. Moore playing 'Gymnopédie.' I know, because she's played it for me, and she told me what it was." She had gone cold from head to foot.

Greg stood up. "Then she's come back, that's all. And we didn't know it."

"But if she's come back, Greg —" It was Paul speaking. "If she's come back, why in the dark? There haven't been any lights."

"And if she's the one playing," said Leslie, so low you could scarcely hear her, "what about the candle?"

It *was* a candle, for the flame, floating about in space, at the same time dipped and wavered. Greg shoved his chair away and started toward the drive, and they all got up and followed, their eyes fixed upon that small light that now hung steadily in the blackness of the upstairs window. They stood close together, looking up through the leaves of the eucalyptus and listening in silence to the slow, plangent tones of the "Gymnopédie."

Then a car slid along the curb, a door slammed, and there were voices.

"But that's —" cried Julia, and they were all running to where they could see Mrs. Moore standing under the street-light giving money to the cabdriver, who now got hold of her bags, one in each hand, and followed her along the walk and up onto the veranda. They moved across the lawn in a little group and when they reached the house steps Julia saw Mrs. Moore fumble in her purse for her key while the cabdriver stood patiently to one side. And at the instant she was about to fit the key into the lock, the door swung wide and there stood Kenny, his mouth open, staring up into Mrs. Moore's face.

For a second he seemed frozen in this position, but turned all at once with a little jerk as though about to race off along the hall and out the back, and Julia was aware of the flickering light behind him as though a candle had been set on the hall table. She heard the "Gymnopédie" still being played and knew then that Kenny had put on a record. In the next instant he had changed his mind and stepped onto the veranda. He was holding out something.

"Here's your key, Mrs. Moore," he said in a light, impudent voice — almost gay, it was. "Julia loaned it to me so I could play a trick." He shoved it into her hand, then flitted off down the steps and away up the street. And Addie streaked after him.

No one said anything, but the next instant Julia was up on the porch standing in front of Mrs. Moore.

"I didn't, Mrs. Moore. I *didn't*. I would *never* have done that. Could I come in and —"

But the woman who stood there, whose face in the half light seemed to Julia as old and as weary as when she had been ill, simply waved her away.

"Not now, dear," she said. "Really, it doesn't matter."

She went in, turned on the hall light, the cabdriver set her bags down inside the door, and she closed it behind him. And when there had been time for her to carry them upstairs, the hall light went out and the house, thereafter, remained in darkness. But Mrs. Moore must have got undressed by firelight, because in a little while Julia saw smoke and sparks going up from the bedroom chimney.

Long after her mother had come upstairs and gone to bed, Julia still twisted and turned, curled and uncurled, but always the vision of Mrs. Moore's closed, indifferent face came between her and sleep.

"Julie?"

"Mom — can't you sleep either?"

"What are you thinking?"

"About Mrs. Moore, because of Ken lying, and how she looked at me. What's happened to her?"

"Something dreadful, apparently. Who's to know? Perhaps we never will."

"What are you thinking about?"

"Ken —"

"I hate him for what he did —"

"There's no need. He's had enough to last a lifetime."

"What d'you expect me to do — love him?"

"No. But I can't think what's to become of him."

"It's his own fault."

"Not entirely. In fact, maybe scarcely at all —"

"But why does he lie?"

"Listen, Julia! If every time you told me the truth about what you'd done, like losing my bread knife or burning the pot roast because you forgot it and it was ruined, or locking Daddy in the woodshed for two and a half hours — if every time you told me the truth, I beat you or cursed you, thereafter you would lie."

Julia had no answer, but after a little:

"He swears — everything he can think of to say. I wouldn't tell you."

"So does his father. That's where he learned it."

"And so you're sorry for him, I'll bet. Mrs. Moore said she's sorry for Mr. Kellerman because he's a failure and so he drinks, and he drinks because he's a failure and his mother's always made excuses for him. That's what she said."

Mrs. Redfern took this in.

"I see what you're thinking. It seems Mrs. Moore and I believe that nobody's to blame for anything, because who knows what the parents did. But there's no point in being alive, it seems to me, if a person never changes. Somehow he has to see himself from the outside —"

"Imagine Mr. Kellerman ever doing that!" exclaimed Julia. "And what about Kenny?"

"Who can imagine? But, actually, playing that little trick, which was rather clever, wasn't what you'd call a crime —"

"Except that he took the key," said Julia, "and lied to Mrs. Moore about me."

"Yes," said her mother, "except for that."

Chapter Thirteen

Julia wrote Rhiannon Moore a note explaining what had happened about the key, but Greg made her write it over because she could not, he said, accuse Ken of having stolen the key when she knew no such thing. She could say he'd probably found it in the door, because it *had* disappeared and he *might* have found it there. But that was all. And she had to rewrite the letter knowing she wouldn't want to ring the bell but would slip it under the door. She felt ashamed and her shame infuriated her, considering what close and happy friends she and Mrs. Moore had been, but she could not, by herself, look at that cold face again knowing she had been careless about the key.

"Would you come with me, Mother, so we could talk to her?" she asked at dinner.

But Mrs. Redfern, strangely preoccupied, only looked up absently and said that she didn't really feel like talking to Rhiannon Moore, nor, after what had happened last night, did she suppose Mrs. Moore would feel like talking to them. The note would do quite well, she said; in fact, she thought Mrs. Moore might prefer it.

Julia stared at her in wordless indignation. It was as if she didn't care a twit about *her,* Julia Redfern, her mother's own child. Mrs. Redfern had got dinner almost in silence, and now ate as if removed from her family, glancing at them only occasionally from some distant, private place. Julia (having almost, but not quite refused dessert) went off full of resentment with her letter.

When she got back, she made out in the swimming dimness of evening someone sitting in the lawn swing and when she went over found that it was Paul. He was sitting in the far corner, almost lost under the shadow of its top, with his feet up and his back against the canvas side. She folded herself in the opposite corner and waited for him to speak. But when he stayed silent:

"What about Ken?" she asked. It was all she could think of to say, when the last person on earth she cared about was Ken Kellerman.

"Gram and my uncle still don't know anything about what happened at Mrs. Moore's, but when Ken didn't come in last night, my aunt knew there was something wrong and got it out of Addie, so now my aunt's mad at him and trying to keep it to herself, and Ken didn't come home to supper. I can't wait to get back up north. I wish we could go home now."

But *I* don't — *I* don't, cried Julia to herself, filled with the same painful longing she had felt only once before in her life: when she knew the moment had come for Greg and her mother and grandparents and herself, aged nine, to come down from their camping place in the mountains, where the solitude had remained unbroken by any human beings but themselves the whole time they had been there, and she had slept out under the trees in a sleeping bag next to Greg and her grandfather. She could not bear to see their clearing in the pines and firs dismantled, to look out of the car and watch the mountains being left behind and foothills taking their place, the little towns with their grubby stores and gas stations, and the fields on the outskirts where old cars were dumped on the banks of choked streams. But they had to come down. They couldn't live in the mountains, Grandfather said. And she hadn't known if she would ever see them again, and never had — not "the real high country," her mother called it, in the same tone of voice she herself would have used. And just as the Berkeley hills were nothing at all like the high country, so there was no one else in the least like Paul, with his smooth brown face and brown hands, and his grave eyes that seemed to hold at times a hidden, quiet humor as if aroused by some secret thought. He had a way of making you feel that it wasn't necessary to be always saying something, that you needn't, as when you were with your own family, say anything at all if you felt quiet.

"Paul, were you afraid last night?"

"No. At least, I don't remember being. I thought maybe Mrs. Moore had died and come back." Yes, underneath everything else, there had been that feeling. "It could happen. I mean it happened to my father. Shall I tell you a kind of ghost story?"

Julia, who a moment before had been filled with sadness, was now as suddenly filled with delight. And as if in answer to her delight Gretchy came out of the dark and leaped up in her lap and settled there, and then Sandy came and crouched in the grass not far away, his paws together, his tail flicking, his eyes two pale green luminous orbs watching them. "A real ghost story?" she asked.

"Oh, yes — it happened. One day," said Paul, in a voice that made of the swing a small room, "I was home alone. And there was a knock at the door and when I went to answer, there was a man standing there who said he was my uncle from India and that he wanted to see my father — he had to talk to him. He told me his name, and it *was* my uncle's, but I'd been told never to let a stranger in the house when my parents were away no matter what he said, so I told him he'd have to come back later. Well, he came that night, and he *was* my uncle, and he said that his wife had died — my mother and father had never seen her — and that he wanted to bring his children over from India so that they could stay with us for a while, if we'd have them, until he could get a job and find a house of his own. And when he said his wife had died I saw the most peculiar look on my father's face, and he asked my uncle if he had a picture of her — of my aunt. And Uncle Dan got out his wallet and handed my father a photograph, and I thought Dad was going to be sick he got so pale." Paul stopped, as though remembering his father's face, and Julia waited.

"But, why?" she asked at last. "Why did he look like that?"

"He told us that the night before, he'd waked up in the dark and seen a woman standing at the foot of the bed and thought it was my mother until he put his arm out and found she was still lying there. And then the woman came toward him, and when she was standing right by the bed, she looked down at him with a kind of anxious, asking look, but didn't say anything, and then faded away. And that was all. Except that when my father saw the photograph, he knew it had been Uncle Dan's wife."

Julia sat silent, thinking, her arms folded around herself to keep from shivering and seeing it all quite clearly just as Paul had described.

"Do you believe he saw her?"

"I don't know. My mother says he was dreaming, but he'd never seen Uncle Dan's wife before. Dad says he knows that what he saw actually happened and that he wasn't asleep."

"And you said in Greg's room, Paul, that when you looked at the painting of Ikhnaton and then at Greg, it made you know everything wasn't ordinary after all. But how could you have said it? Everything keeps seeming anything *but* ordinary to me — I mean, little things, too, not even the big things like Greg and Ikhnaton, and your father waking up in the night and then seeing the photograph. Does it seem ordinary to you to go camping up in the high mountains and see all those wild animals?"

Paul shook his head.

"No. Camping — I wait for that all year. That's the real time. That's where we're going when we get home."

And suddenly, as if the thought were too much for him, he swung his feet down, and leaned over and held his hand out to Sandy. And Sandy, seeing a moth spin up from the dark grass, leaped for it — high in the air — and Gretchy jumped down and leaped for Sandy, and then for the moth, and another moth. And there on the shadowy stage of the grass that gave off scattered points of light from drops of dew reflecting Daddy's lamp on one side and Mrs. Moore's on the other, as though minute jewels had been lost here and there, the cats chased and leaped in utter silence. Twisting, pirouetting on feet that seemed scarcely to touch the earth, Gretchy was a half-seen darting shape and Sandy a swift, mad ghost, both drunk with the joy of night and the movement of flitting specks of white that drifted always just beyond paw-reach. It was a ballet — a cat ballet that, no sooner begun, Julia remembered afterwards, seemed to end. For now Gretchy disappeared, and Sandy after her.

And they did not come back, though Paul and Julia waited without moving. It had been what Mrs. Moore would have called — that word she had used the night she and Julia heard the birds migrating high overhead in their multitudes. It was a word that meant some perfect coming together of happenings that might never occur in just that way again, and for Julia it was this: Paul being here and talking quietly in the small room of the swing, and then the cats dancing their ballet, something she had never seen them do before.

Paul got up and started across the lawn and Julia followed after. She did not know what made her ask the next question. It seemed to be asked of its own accord before she could stop it.

"Paul, why did you come?"

"Because tomorrow we're leaving —"

"But you'll come back?"

"No, I don't think so. Mother and Dad don't like it here."

They stood now at the end of the driveway, but still in shadow, and Julia had to make herself ask the next question.

"Would you write to me?"

His hands were in his pockets; he was half turned away as if in his mind he was already on the way home, going north.

"What's the use of promising? I know I wouldn't — I never write letters." And then he turned and looked at her and took his hands out of his pockets. He rested them on her shoulders, leaned over and quickly, lightly, she felt his lips brush her cheek. "Good-bye, Julia," he said, and then was gone. And she did not even step out beyond

Mrs. Moore's hedge to watch him go, because what would have been the use?

She ran, with her head down, as fast as her legs would take her, back along the drive, across the grass, up on the porch, in the front door, past her mother who was sitting reading in the brown leather chair, and up the stairs to her own dark room. And there she was, lying with her face in the pillow, when her mother came in and shut the door behind her.

"Julie, what is it? Did you talk to Mrs. Moore? Is she angry with you?" But Julia could not answer, and her mother sat down on the bed and did not say anything for several minutes, waiting for her to speak. And at last:

"It's Paul — he's gone —"

"But he'll come back."

"No, he never will. His parents say they won't."

She felt her mother's hand on her arm, and then it was taken away. And after another silence:

"Julia, I think I must tell you something. Perhaps you'll understand now, at least a little because of Paul and because he means something special to you. I'm in love with Uncle Phil and he with me, and we want to be married. The house is almost finished. We'd live up there."

Julia had stopped breathing.

"But what about my father!"

"Julia, he's dead. I don't have him — I don't have a husband, and you and Greg have no father. You and I happened to one another, and we love one another, but we didn't choose. Now I've chosen someone and he has chosen me. To others, if not to you, I'm still young — I'm thirty-five and I have most of my life ahead of me. Will you try to understand that I must have someone besides my children, and I want Uncle Phil —"

"But you can't!" cried Julia in a rage of despair, turning over and staring up at her mother. "You *can't* — how *can* you — *That* One! He's *nothing* like my father —"

"I know. He is simply himself, loving and kind, as he has been to you. I feel peaceful with him. I wouldn't want him like your father."

"But what do you *mean?* How can you say that? Didn't you love him?"

"Yes — yes, I did, Julia. But your father was a very difficult person to love. You must understand that. So often I wasn't happy —"

"He was handsome —"

"What has that to do with *anything!* This picture you so carefully keep on your desk these days is a glamorized photographer's picture. And what can you really remember, Julia? He was hardly ever with us — always away because of some new project that was going to put us on 'easy street' — how many times he said it! And then when he was home he was forever shutting himself off from us, trying to write and never succeeding because whatever he wrote was never quite what anybody wanted. What *do* you remember?"

"Everything — everything! I remember when he used to take me down to the wharves at the bay across the huge fields where the cows were and I loved the smell of the bay and the tarry smell of the wharves where they had the big barrels with shrimps in them. And we'd buy a bag of shrimps that had just been cooked, and somewhere else, at a little store on the way home, we'd get watercress and it would be in the evening when everything smelled good, and he'd always have to tell me to be careful not to step in the cow pats because I wouldn't notice them. And when we'd get home, he'd build a big fire in the fireplace, and you'd make tea and we'd have toast and shrimps and watercress and you used to say, 'Now I'm happy!' Do you remember *that?"*

"Of course I remember! Of course I do! There *were* times when I was happy. But not often — not often! And, Julia —"

"And do you remember," cried Julia, "that we used to go up in the hills and my father would pick flowers for you and you always used to laugh because he would cut off their stems absolutely even? And when we got home you would sit in the brown leather chair and he would take off your shoes and rub your feet because they were tired —"

"Yes — yes!" All at once her mother got up and began walking back and forth with her arms folded and her hands clasping her elbows as if she were cold. "He could do that, and yet — yet he could get into such a temper that he picked up your little cat —"

"He *didn't* — it was the boys who did that. I remember, because I saw them —"

"No, Julia, it wasn't —"

"But he loved my cat —"

"Yes, in whatever way he could." Now her mother was standing at the window, looking out, perhaps seeing nothing, and it seemed almost as if she were talking to herself. "And he loved you, but when I gave you that big doll for Christmas and left it sitting beside your bed for you to find Christmas morning, you woke up in the night and its glass eyes had come loose, and when you tried to fix them, they fell back inside the head, and you were terrified. And you wouldn't come in and tell me for fear of waking your father —"

"I *could* have gone in — I *could* have! And it would have been all right. We used to go for walks after dinner sometimes, and he would tell me about when he was a little boy, that there was a swamp near his house in England, and the bull frogs would say, 'Better go round, better go round, better go round,' and the tree frogs, 'Pretty deep, pretty deep, pretty deep' —"

"Yes — yes, I know."

"I remember everything he told me — everything." Yes, she remembered. And other happenings as well, darker ones that she pushed away and would not confess, yet if they're inside yourself, you can't help seeing them. All the same, suddenly she took the picture from her desk and held it in her lap and put a hand on it. "I will not leave this house, and I will not have That One for a father. Not ever."

And her mother turned and went downstairs, and after Julia was in bed, came up much later but did not come

near, only went into her own room and closed the door —
a thing she never did. And Julia wanted to get up and open
it and say something, to go over and touch her and maybe
crawl into bed beside her to catch her warm scent. She
never used perfume; why, then, was there always a faint
fragrance about her? But Julia could not make herself
move or say anything.

Chapter Fourteen

Mrs. Redfern got up early, had breakfast with Greg, and left before Julia was up. Julia heard the front door close and ran out onto the balcony to watch her go, walking slowly, her head down as if she were lost in thought. Julia still could not speak, though she tried; she wanted intensely to see her mother turn, wanted some sign to be given. But Mrs. Redfern rounded the corner onto the drive, and Julia went inside and listened; the whole place was quiet. Greg, too, must have gone off. "Greg?" she called at the top of the stairs. Yes, he had.

After breakfast, during which she had the pleasure of reading without interruption, and of eating, unreproached, five slices of toast covered far too thickly with butter and strawberry jam, Julia began copying "The Mask" in her neatest hand for *St. Nicholas.* When she had finished, she put it back into its envelope, by this time worn and soiled, with one large and two small grease spots on it, sealed it up, wrote out another address label, and took it to the post office to be sent off. After seeing it tossed indifferently into some invisible bin as though it were nothing but an ordinary piece of mail, Julia turned away, washed by a wave of bleak boredom. "What now — what now?" She might go home and finish "The Harpet," but her story had paled lately in comparison with life itself, so that the idea of it no longer flew about in her mind in that tantalizing, compelling way that leaves no alternative to putting it onto paper. Daddy Chandler would be working at his desk. If she went to Addie's, Ken might be there, or Paul would probably just be leaving and they would be wordless so that last night would be ruined. She wanted nothing to touch or to change what she already had of him.

She hovered at the door of the Japanese shop to catch that intoxicating smell which was probably a mingling, her mother had said once, of the straw matting they had on the floors, of lacquer and sandalwood and teak and of the incense they always burned. It drew her time and again on her way home from school into that burnished interior. Here she wandered undisturbed by any questions from the small Japanese gentleman in charge, who never hovered but simply nodded to her from behind the jewelry case and went on smoking and reading his newspaper covered with squiggles that went up and down instead of across. He knew she never touched anything, but feasted her eyes on the flowered robes, the brocades woven of purple and silver and cinnabar and imperial yellow, the lacquer boxes with their patterns of gold leaves and branches and birds, the numberless objects so delicate, so miraculous it seemed they must have been fashioned by fingers not human. He knew that she wanted to stand, lost to reality, in front of that minute scene contained in a bowl planted with moss hills, a glade of trees three inches high, a temple, and a lake, no bigger than the palm of Julia's hand, with a bridge over it. You had only to gaze steadily for a second or two, she had found, to become one of those figures under the trees about to wander across the moss into the temple, inside of which could be glimpsed a golden Buddha that turned out, when you swelled back into the giant world again, to be about the size of your littlest fingernail.

But the Japanese shop was for unreflecting happiness and contentment. She had now in mind, suddenly, that dark hollow, pervaded by an acrid odor of rat, that underlay the music store where her mother worked and that had as its neighbor the basement of a Greek restaurant. There was an old organ down there and what she needed was to sit in the half dark, pumping with her feet at the resisting pedals and making a mournful tune creep out, a tune like the voice of some mad Ophelia, for she could no more play the organ than she could play the piano at Gram Kellerman's or Mrs. de Rizzio's. Yet there were times when the gloom and the cold and the sad sound of the organ could be a kind of melancholy comfort.

She greeted with a thump on its head the big white papier-mâché Victor dog, almost as tall as herself, that always stood at the entrance to the music store. Its head was tilted, with its left ear up, as though listening for the dulcet strains of some Victor record to come wafting out, but all it was catching at the moment was the conversation of two women. "— then you turn it over," one of them said as she passed Julia, "and put a cherry in the middle, and it looks just bee-*ew*-deeful —" Puzzle: what do you turn over, put a cherry in the middle of it, and it looks just bee-*ew*-deeful? She'd try that one on Addie. Then she looked up and saw her mother searching through the record rack for something for an old, old man who seemed to be smelling the records he had in his hands. Julia's heart lifted, for the thought all at once occurred to her that they might have lunch together, she and her mother, so that she felt almost gay as she walked along the aisle paneled on either hand with enormous framed photographs of the great men and women of the Golden Age of opera: Galli-Curci, Enrico Caruso, Alma Gluck, Schumann-Heink and, there at the end, Tetrazzini, who possessed an exceedingly large bust. It was even larger than Aunt Alex's, who quite often wore a string of amber beads that lay along the top and then plunged, swinging, over the precipice. Tetrazzini, tightly encased in lamé, also had a string of beads that plunged and swung, but they looked to be diamonds as big as cranberries.

Julia sent her mother an intimate, confiding smile that said, "I have forgiven you — let's be friends," but Mrs.

Redfern only glanced at her, frowned slightly, and turned away. Presently, as she walked past:

"What is it, Julia?"

"I thought — could we have lunch?"

"No. Uncle Phil wants me to have it with him. You'd better run along home and get something." Then she went into That One's office.

A kind of pain began at once to spread from that always sensitive, too responsive center, Julia's stomach, and she recognized it at once, her old enemy that always came at the call of some sudden rebuff or humiliation. She stayed where she was until Miss Umphelby, who was probably a thousand years old, came out to relieve Mrs. Redfern at the counter and began a low, absorbed conversation with the old man. Julia slipped over to the basement door, closed it behind her and allowed herself the horror of half a second of enveloping, stone-cold, rat-smelling darkness. You are locked in a dungeon, she told herself sternly — then quick, turned on the naked light bulb that hung over the stairs.

She descended, listening for scutterings, and wedged her way past crates and packing cases to where the old organ sat in an island of gloom. It was fancy as a wedding cake and coated with dust over which were sprinkled rat pellets. Julia carelessly swept these from the keys with a fistful of excelsior and dragged over the box she kept hidden under a pile of rubbish because it was exactly the right height to sit on. She was still for a moment, testing the pain in her stomach to determine if it might be going away, then began pumping on the foot pedals and pressing down keys in chords, which brought forth a most entrancing, reedy mingling of tones. Now the dim basement with its covey of horned and jagged shadows faded away and a story began its accompanying life to the music.

Above each group of keys on the board were circlets of ivory on which were engraved in black in a precise and elegant hand such fascinating words as Open Diapason, Stopped Diapason, Vox Humana, Gamba, Corno di Bassetto, Vox Angelica, Bourdon and Dulciana. These curious and flowing names had always given Julia, when she murmured them over, the sense of having come from some antique land where gentlemen wore doublets of satin or velvet and the ladies tall, pointed headdresses from which veils floated. And always, as she played, the echoes of the names threaded themselves through the tremulous voice of the organ so that the evocation of that land was part of her playing. At length, after several others, the story of the imprisoned nuns she had told Paul began unfolding, as it had many times before, and so vivid was the scene before her that it did not matter where she put her hands. The breathy wail she was bringing forth was all she needed to transport her to that stone tower where the two incarcerated ones listened to the life of the world going by unaware, far below.

But now, as she paused to create some new turn of events, she heard a voice from the direction of the stairs.

"— then why not do her the honor of letting her contend with a difficulty or two for a change, some real diffi-

culty, instead of arranging everything for her pleasure no
matter what happens to *us!*" It was Uncle Phil and he was
coming down. "The completely fatuous parent," he said.
"No one else matters, only that child —"

"You don't understand me at all, do you, Phil?" There
came the click of a woman's heels on the cement steps;
the basement door closed and the sounds of the world upstairs, voices, records playing in a kind of insane cacoph-
ony, someone vamping "Roses of Picardy" on a piano,
someone laughing, all were shut away. "Fatuous parent!
It's *not* my trying to arrange everything for her pleasure
that's made me decide. It's her utter rejection, and it won't
change. I couldn't live with it — with that grinding un-
happiness. How little you know me, *really*." Julia sat
motionless, then leaned backward enough to be able to
peer out. Uncle Phil stood at the bottom of the stairs, her
mother three or four steps above. The naked light shone
on their heads; they stood in a glare of bluish-white and
behind them, beyond the stairs, was a jumble of half-
seen shapes. "I thought that you, of all people, understood
me. But not at all — not at all. You don't even begin
to —"

"No," said Uncle Phil in a strange, cold, remote voice
Julia had never heard before, "apparently I don't."

Celia Redfern turned and went back up again. "Well,
then," came her level, clipped reply, "that's that."

And the door at the top opened, Uncle Phil stayed where
he was for a moment and then followed, and the door
closed. Julia, terrified, slipped out along her path between

the packing cases but caught herself at the foot of the stairs. She could not go up — not now. She would have to escape out the back, past the repairman's bench covered with coiled springs and tools and cans of graphite, and into the narrow alley where the rubbish men came to empty the barrels.

But now the door up there opened again and before she had the presence of mind to dart back under cover, Uncle Phil came running down. She stared up at him, unable to move because of the expression on his face, an expression of blind, frozen anguish. But she had no need to move. He seemed not to see her. His hand went out and he appeared to feel nothing as he brushed her aside and strode, stabbed his way into the dark among those piled shapes. In a moment she heard the alley door slam.

On shaking legs Julia stole along her secret path and sank down in front of the organ. After a while, after perhaps five or ten minutes, someone — Miss Umphelby, it must have been, because of the slipping sound of flat shoes — someone came halfway down the stairs, listened, and then went up again and turned off the light. And Julia, in that fearful, overpowering darkness full of rustlings and small, quick scratchings, made her way to the alley door, stepped outside, looked up and down, and went home.

Around six that evening, she did the breakfast dishes and set the table for dinner, peeled the potatoes and put them on to boil, as well as another pan of water for whatever vegetable her mother might bring. But when Mrs. Redfern came, she had brought nothing and went directly upstairs and shut her door; Julia followed, but she did not, somehow, dare to open it and go in. There was a feeling she had that if she did, the news might be plain on her face that she knew quite well why her mother was not saying anything nor getting dinner ready as she always did no matter what had happened.

"Mother?" said Julia in a stifled voice.

"I want to speak to you," her mother said.

Julia, quaking, opened the door. How could her mother have known? What *did* she know?

"Julia," said Mrs. Redfern, and she was lying on the bed with an arm across her eyes, "I've phoned your Aunt Alex, and Greg will take you across to San Francisco tomorrow after lunch. You'll be staying there for a while."

Julia turned this over in her mind. "But, why?"

Her mother did not answer at once. Then, "Go down now and fix Greg and yourself some dinner. He'll be home pretty soon."

"But what about you?"

"Just please close the door and go downstairs."

Chapter Fifteen

She could not, of course, leave for San Francisco without saying good-bye to Daddy Chandler. But there was no joyful racing up his stairs this time, for she did not know what he knew, nor what the de Rizzios knew. When their kitchen door opened and little Mrs. de Rizzio came out and caught sight of her hovering there, her stomach gave a kind of lurch.

"Why, hel-*lo,* Julia. You going up to see Daddy already? I think he'll still be working." She'd been told nothing, then, Julia saw in her expression. Complete innocence was in her face, nothing but her usual, warm, rather teasing affection with not so much as a hint of reproach or disapproval.

"I'm going up to say good-bye." Julia put a certain grave tone into her voice.

"Good-*bye*! But where are you off to? Your mother hasn't decided to move — you're not —"

"Oh, no! We certainly are not moving, Mrs. de Rizzio. Not ever that. It's just that I'm going over to stay with Aunt Alex and Uncle Hugh for a while. So I have to tell Daddy —" And suddenly she ran down and flung her arms around Mrs. de Rizzio with such intensity that the little woman tottered.

"*Gra*cious, child! What a bear you are! Or, what is it your mother calls you? 'My wild pony.' That's it!" Mrs. de Rizzio made scattered attempts to straighten her piled hair. "Now you have a fine time, dearie. It'll be splendid visiting over there — they're quite well off, aren't they?" Her blue eyes sparkled with amused irony.

"Yep," said Julia indifferently. "They are. I like Uncle Hugh best." She kissed Mrs. de Rizzio, then turned and went up. As always, she opened the door softly so as to be able to play her little joke, but could not, for some reason, contain a sudden mysterious upwelling of glee. All was well, really — wasn't it? The family was safe, her mother having said, there at the top of the basement stairs at the music store, "Then that's that," in a flat, finished-off voice. They *were* staying. And her mother would be herself again in a little while, by the time Julia got back. In fact, surely it was what she was determined to be, her usual self — but she needed time. And meanwhile, over in the city, she and Uncle Hugh would have fun, and maybe he would take her to a play instead of a picture show; possibly even two plays.

"Daddy Chandler!" She stood watching him, scratching away on one of those long sheets of paper. And he turned, and took off his glasses and wiped them and rubbed his eyes. Then he laughed to himself and held out his hand for her to come over. She settled on his knee with her arm around his neck, sniffed his eau de cologne, and looked at him. "I have some news for you, Daddy," she said, her face somber, her tone solemn, full of portent.

"Is it good news, Julia?" He put his glasses on again and regarded her. How she loved him, she thought, with a sudden, curious dart of something like — but it was too glancing and quick to name.

"I'm going away," she said quietly, looking down at the front of her good dress with a rich appreciation of the moment. "I'm going away to the city."

Daddy Chandler gazed at her, startled. "Going away?" he queried in an odd tone. "How's that?" The effect on him had been all she could have desired, simply because of the way she'd told him.

"Oh, not forever — don't look so tragic! Only for a few days, maybe a week. To stay with Uncle Hugh and Aunt Alex."

"She's the large one, isn't she?" She'd come here once and Daddy had met her, and she had told him without letup all about her girlhood in San Francisco. He chuckled suddenly, wickedly, as though remembering something, and then they were both laughing, though about what

Julia wasn't sure — maybe Aunt Alex's solidity, her enormous dignity, her vast satisfaction with herself.

Then here came Greg. "Jule! Ju-li-a — we'll miss the train!"

"Good-bye, Daddy. I'll write — I promise you I will — a card anyway — good-bye —"

She ran to the door and looked back. He was smiling at her. His arm went up. She blew him a kiss and was off down the stairs. She had already bid Gretchy and Sandy a fond farewell, and they sat now side by side, front paws together, tails curled round, at the head of the driveway watching her go. She had her purse, and her decent coat was over her arm. Greg had her suitcase. She still had not seen Mrs. Moore and though she looked up at the windows of the red house with hope, no curtain drew aside nor even so much as stirred.

Right in the middle of the tracks on Shattuck Avenue a car had stalled. The driver got out and pushed fiercely, for the train was waiting. Julia and Greg got on, and presently the Southern Pacific pulled out of the station with leisurely grandeur, slowly gathering speed on its way to meet the ferry at the pier. Greg didn't say much. He read his book and Julia thought. She thought about Mrs. Moore and of how, once upon a time — only a few weeks ago — she could have gone over and told her the whole thing, about her mother and Uncle Phil, and it would have helped. They could have talked it all out. But not now — not now. Maybe they could never talk again. She had not even seen

Rhiannon Moore once since she had come home the night of Greg's birthday party, and Mrs. Moore did not any longer play the piano. Mrs. de Rizzio said that she was suffering from migraine again.

At the pier, Greg and Julia crossed the gangplank where a man in dirty trousers stood watching the crowd of commuters with a superior expression on his face and a hawser in his stubbed hands. They could not get under way without him, he seemed to be saying with that expression of his, because *he* had control of the rope mooring them to the stanchion. Julia and Greg made a tour of the ferry to see if anything was different from last time, then went out on the forward deck to stand at the rail and look across the cold bottle-green water at that far city on the opposite shore. And when the boat horn gave its shattering bellow, Julia's heart leaped like a stricken frog and her stomach felt wrenched, though she knew perfectly well the bellow was coming. Now they watched in silence while the pilings, not four feet away, gray, splintered, chalked white on top with gull droppings, leaned and groaned as though at the limit of endurance while the ferry gradually drew itself out amidst a great churning and foaming.

Over to one side and ahead of the boat a broken carpet of dancing, blinding sunlight stretched away. A branch with all its green leaves on it washed by, together with bits of orange peel and some broken pieces of crate. Gulls swept up in an excited cloud — like a fling of white paper scraps, Julia thought — and uttering melancholy cries of "Chark! Chark!" they streamed forward on wings that were

snowy underneath and dark gray on top with a neat pip-
ing of white along the edges. They turned their smooth
white heads to regard the deck passengers out of expres-
sionless eyes while resting comfortably on invisible rivers
of air, pink feet tucked back, tilting and planing down for
chunks of dry bread the shouting children tossed up from
brown paper bags.

But Julia had forgotten hers. It was a thing she had
never done, not once in all the years she had been going
over.

"And why am I, Greg?" she asked suddenly. "Why am
I going to stay at Uncle Hugh's and Aunt Alex's?"

"So Mom can think."

Think! "But what *about?*" Oh, it was like the boat horn
bellowing, the shock of it. "Do you mean it isn't settled,
then? Why, yesterday afternoon — I — I mean, we're not
going up *there,* are we? Up on the hill?" She pressed close
to him, watching his face, and she saw a muscle in his
cheek move. He straightened his glasses.

"You know, Jule, you're always having a fit about
people being cruel to animals, not caring, and yet *you*
don't care a snap of your finger about Mom. You don't
care how she feels, or whether she'll ever be happy. All
you care about is yourself —"

"Well, she cares about *her*self —"

"But about us, too. She wants a whole family."

"But she's *got* one," cried Julia. "She's *got* one. Why
would she want anyone else? We were perfectly happy

before all this Uncle Phil business began. Besides, there's my father — ours, I mean. She *can't* just forget him."

Greg didn't answer for a moment, only stood staring out over the water. "You know what you are?" he said presently in a cool, almost gentle voice. "You're a hypocrite. What do you really care about Dad, and about Mom staying faithful to his memory? I'll tell you what I think. I think that all this going on about him and keeping his picture on your desk where you can see it last thing at night and the first thing in the morning is pure bilge. Why do you keep it there? *You* know — to ward off anything that could happen that might disarrange your nice private little world. You've only had it there for the last few months. What you really want, actually, is just to keep that room of yours — and that's *all* you want —"

"And Daddy Chandler and the de Rizzios and Mrs. Moore," exclaimed Julia, wrapped away inside her own passion. "And Addie. And I *hate* the new house — I absolutely *loathe* it, nothing but a stucco box perched up there on the hill." Her room! Her room! To hide her face, she dropped it on her arms, crossed on the rail. And when she looked up again, Greg had left her and was sitting over on the other side of the deck, turned away. After a while she went and sat beside him, and when he did not notice her, she touched his arm. "Greg, what about my father? *Was* he a real writer?"

"He tried to be," said Greg, "but never had a single thing published in his whole life, no matter what he wrote."

Julia saw in her mind the face of that man smiling out of the picture (but the eyes, she had often thought, were not really smiling), who had spent his life in doing something he loved but who had never succeeded. "Maybe it would be better if I didn't try —"

"If you have to, you will. If there's something you must do, you do it — it's as if it's handed to you."

"Like my father handing me the mask. He handed me his," said Julia without thinking. Then she looked up, her eyes widening. Why, what had she meant? It was her dream.

Aunt Alex, when she had been forty pounds lighter, had been very beautiful, but now, enamored of food, was bolster-shaped with a face like a large, ripe, golden peach. "When she tells a recipe and says, 'Take a cup of butter,' " Julia had confided to Addie, "I feel like going and eating celery." And Aunt Alex was always telling recipes, her plump, smooth hands, with their rosy nails, moving in the air as though she were shaping each spoonful and carrying it lovingly to the bowl.

She continually bossed Uncle Hugh, who appeared to take no notice but who usually did what she wanted, and this made Julia furious. After their father had been killed in the war, Uncle Hugh now and then took Julia and Greg to lunch in the city at the Green Door, which you went up to in an elevator and where they served popovers as big as baseballs, and then afterwards they would go out to the museum in Golden Gate Park. What fun they al-

ways had! Sometimes Uncle Hugh would sing in an ex-
aggerated baritone with his chin in, as though he were a
great opera singer, "What are the wild waves saying,
sister dear, all the day long —?" and the answer was "Try
Beecham's pills!" Julia and he had their own stories and
laughed over their own private jokes. Yet once or twice,
now that she was no longer a mere blind child, she had felt
a kind of silence in him, something he never said anything
about but that seemed to brood under his teasing and
cheeriness.

But how pleased he was to see them both when he
opened the door. He put an arm across Greg's shoulder
and then caught up Julia and whirled her around and
around the living room. "A ton!" he cried. "You weigh a
ton, Julia! No pie and ice cream tonight, and Hulda's
made apricot, just specially for you —" She didn't care a
bit how he teased her, it was so exciting to see him again.
He was tall and firm and his suits fitted him beautifully.
She very much admired the way he looked, with his hair
just turning gray.

As for Aunt Alex, she could not understand why Greg
wouldn't stay for dinner. She doted on him and invariably
felt called upon to remind Celia Redfern of his virtues.
"A *great* credit to you, Celia!" she would always say, as
if convinced his mother did not at all deserve him. "You
should be enormously proud of that boy," she directed
with authority.

"Well, I'm not," Mrs. Redfern would answer, one eyebrow lifting in a way she had. "Not in the least. He's a

burden and a trial, with his everlasting junk and his messiness and his unmade bed and the dust lying around an inch thick because no one's supposed to move anything. He's nothing but a boy with a book, of no use to anyone."

This shocked Aunt Alex to the heart.

"Celia! I must say I do not understand you. To say that in front of him —"

"I am, in fact, deeply wounded," and Greg would adjust his glasses, gaze at Aunt Alex, and look solemn.

But Aunt Alex had no sense of humor; she never laughed at other people's jokes, only her own. She stood now at Greg's elbow where he hovered, half in the living room, half in the hall, ready to leave at the first opportunity, and she had her arm hooked through his and was patting him and pressing him to tell her all about his girls. And Greg, who couldn't stand being doted on and pressed and patted and buttonholed, presently sleeked away and Julia knew exactly where he was headed for: a certain little secondhand bookshop he had discovered — Schoolworthy's — over near Telegraph Hill. He'd go home burdened as usual with more of his dusty, boring old books on Egypt with the little tiny print and the diagrams. She herself went out into the kitchen to give Hulda a hug and to have a sniff of the pie, which was even now baking in the oven and sending out a fragrance of crust and hot fruit. Then she went back to the living room and sat on a footstool near the fireplace that had a Grecian column on either side of it and told Uncle Hugh almost all that had happened to her since the last time she saw

him. And he didn't mind at all if she poked up the fire and
fed it even when it was hardly necessary. The flames made
a kind of quiet, rippling sound and there was a big silver
bowl of roses up on the mantel whose scent she could
smell while they talked. It was very peaceful — Aunt Alex
was off upstairs somewhere writing letters.

At dinner there seemed to be some difficulty about
tickets Uncle Hugh had bought. He'd got three so that
Julia could go. Aunt Alex patiently put down her napkin
(the table napkins at Aunt Alex's were always so large
and thick and glossy — "intimidating," Greg called them
— that you could scarcely bear to use them for fear of
making some vulgar spot). She gazed at her husband.

"But I told you, Hugh, that it simply isn't a play for a
child. Well, it only means that we shall have to leave her
with Hulda. The situation of Davidson and Sadie, of
course — you must see my point. No, it's quite impossible.
I will not take the responsibility. Besides, the Whitings
will be there and we could all go out somewhere afterwards, which we certainly wouldn't if —" There was no
need to finish. Aunt Alex turned her head and looked out
comfortably over the lights of San Francisco (spread for
her special benefit, you couldn't help thinking) with the
air of having considered and closed a matter that had not
been very weighty in the first place. Now she plunged her
fork into the apricot pie and Uncle Hugh frowned and
twiddled his napkin ring round his first finger.

"Tell you what, Julia," he said. "*Romeo and Juliet*'s
playing at the Alcazar and I could get tickets for that for

tomorrow night, I'm pretty sure. It'll have to be then, because that's the last —"

"But, no, Hugh," put in Aunt Alex, her fork poised.
"Oren Moore's tomorrow night. How could you forget!"

Something grew still inside of Julia.

"Did you say Oren Moore?" Her eyes went from Aunt
Alex's face to Uncle Hugh's. "He's here now — in San
Francisco?"

"You mean you didn't *know?*" exclaimed Aunt Alex in
mock astonishment. Then she was serious. "Now tell me
honestly, Julia Redfern," she said, "have you ever actually
heard of Oren Moore? Do you know the least thing about
him? Or are you just showing off, as I've known you to
do — *and* fabricate!"

"I've more than just heard of him," said Julia, staring
up sideways at Aunt Alex.

"Well, what can *that* mean? Who is he, then?"

"A piano player. Famous. I mean, he plays all over the
world and he lives in Ireland. His mother is a very close
friend of mine."

Aunt Alex was silent for a moment. Then, "In-*deed*,"
she breathed. You could see she didn't believe a word
about the friend part.

But Julia, all at once, was no longer at the dinner table.
She was up in the music room with Rhiannon Moore, who
was saying, "And when Oren comes, in a month or two,
you and I will go over together and hear him. I promise
you we will." But had she ever really, Julia asked herself,
believed that promise? "Well, maybe only sometimes,"

she said thoughtfully. "How long will he be here, Uncle Hugh?"

"Just tonight and tomorrow night. A very limited engagement. And, Alex, I meant to tell you —" Here Uncle Hugh hesitated, and Julia noticed a tight look at the outer corners of his eyes.

Aunt Alex's hand dropped with a thud on the table. "Hugh! Don't *tell* me you didn't get tickets —"

"I couldn't, Alex. They'd been sold out for days —"

"But I *asked* you two weeks ago! Oh, I *think* that is simply inexcusable. Oren Moore! And here I've been looking forward — absolutely de*pend*ing upon it that you had —"

And then the phone rang. And Aunt Alex flung herself back in her chair, her big velvety eyes blazing, while Uncle Hugh got up and hurried toward the hall as if escaping the wrath of the gods, or rather of one particular goddess. As both the dining room and the hall were lengthy, Julia and Aunt Alex couldn't quite hear what was being said and sat boxed together in a strained,· awkward silence. When he came back, his face bore a peculiar expression and he seemed to glisten with pleasure.

"Julia," he said, "it's for you. The lady said to tell you that it's Mrs. Rhiannon Moore calling. What a mellifluous name — don't you agree, Alex?" and he sent her a cheery smile. But the look she gave back was both cold and piercing, and it said that she suspected him of some low, shabby trick.

"Hello, Mrs. Moore?" said Julia out in the hall in a high, uncertain tone as if she wasn't at all sure that anyone was actually at the other end of the line.

"Julia, my dear," came Rhiannon Moore's voice with its husky burr, "thank heaven you're there and not gone off someplace. I didn't see you leave today, and if I hadn't been able to get hold of you after my promise, I'd never have forgiven myself. Oren's playing, and he's been able to get me two tickets for tomorrow night. I wasn't at all sure he could get any because they were sold out so far in advance but somehow he has two box seats for us. Will you be able to go?"

"Oh, Mrs. Moore — oh, of course I'll be able to —"

"Good — good! Then I shall come by in a cab for you tomorrow night at eight. And you will be ready, won't you? Don't trouble about what to wear, in case you didn't bring any dress-up things —"

"Oh, but I have — I thought maybe we'd be going out, I mean Uncle Hugh and Aunt Alex and me, and I'll be ready."

"At eight, then Julia. And I have so much to explain. It's been a rather difficult time. Good-bye, dear."

"Good-bye, Mrs. Moore."

Julia went back to the dining room in a daze of joy and gazed, ecstatic, at Aunt Alex. Uncle Hugh had his back to the room, standing at the bay windows with his coffee. Now he turned.

"It *was* Oren's mother, Aunt Alex," said Julia. "It *was* Mrs. Rhiannon Moore. And we *are* going to hear him play. She's coming by for me in a taxi tomorrow night at eight and I'm to be ready. And just to think," she said in wonderment, "that I didn't really believe her!" Aunt Alex was sitting bolt upright staring at Julia. She seemed, still, to be unable to find anything to say. And all at once, overcome with bliss, Julia made for Uncle Hugh who, luckily, had put down his cup and saucer. "Uncle Hugh, Uncle Hugh —" and she threw her arms around his neck and swung. "What do you turn over, put a cherry in the middle of it, and it looks just bee-*ew*-deeful?"

"Give up," laughed Uncle Hugh. "Give up, Julia. What *do* you turn over, put a cherry in the middle of it, and it looks just bee-*ew*-deeful?"

"Why, an upside-down cake, of course," said Aunt Alex, not in the least amused. "But why must you pronounce the word 'beautiful' in that bar*bar*ic fashion?"

Chapter Sixteen

Aunt Alex, having been shown Julia's good dress, would
not hear of its being worn to the concert. It might be quite
satisfactory, she said, for a children's party or to go shop-
ping in. But it definitely would not do to go with Oren
Moore's mother to hear Oren Moore at the Tivoli.

"But do you mean, then," wailed Julia in unbelieving
horror, "that I'm not *going?*"

"Don't be absurd, child. Of course you're going. I'm
simply saying that we shall have to get you something
else to wear. And we can thank our stars that your coat's
black — I would say that it's presentable. Now show me
your shoes. Yes, the usual thing — patent leather. Well,
they won't be too much seen, and I can loan you a plain
black evening purse and we can go over my jewelry for

something unpretentious. I have a short string of quite good small pearls."

These decisions made, they got into Aunt Alex's car and drove down into the city to one of the better department stores, where Aunt Alex chose what she called "an appropriate and attractive" dress. Luckily, Julia also thought it appropriate and attractive: a dusty pink velvet, plain but well cut. For the first time since she could remember, Julia felt she looked the way she'd often longed to look, slim and somewhat older than she was. To tell the truth, she didn't just *like* the dress, she was crazy about it. Oh, wait till Addie saw! Wait till Addie heard all about everything! But then, just as the saleslady was about to get it ready to be taken home, Julia had a thought.

"Aunt Alex," she said, "is it an expensive dress? It looks terribly expensive."

Aunt Alex, who was sitting on a little white and gold chair directing operations, flapping her long kid gloves against her knee and occasionally tucking her back hair more firmly into place, raised both eyebrows.

"Why do you ask?"

"Well, because I — because my mother — I mean I'm not sure my mother could af —"

"But she has nothing to do with this. Nothing at all." Suddenly Aunt Alex gave Julia an odd, down-twisting smile. "Are you pleased with it?"

"It's the *most* wonderful dress," said Julia, standing in front of Aunt Alex with her hands clasped together, "that I've ever had in my whole life."

Now Julia was sitting with Rhiannon Moore in what
Mrs. Moore said was a box — a kind of outcropping on
the side of the theatre down at the front near the stage
and slightly lower than the first balcony, a small, open-
fronted room with chairs in it. The instant she and Mrs.
Moore entered, Julia recognized it at once as the kind of
place Abraham Lincoln had been shot in and where kings
and queens and their progeny sit at plays and ballets and
operas. When the royal family enters, the whole audience
rises to greet its sovereigns, and the king and queen and
their children bow and make gracious gestures of acceptance of this public homage. Then the audience, diamonds
and rubies and emeralds flashing here and there as the
women turn, sits down again with rustlings and murmurings. And everyone begins passing comments in low voices
about how royalty is looking this evening and about the
queen's and the princesses' gowns and jewels.

Of course most of this audience never even lifted their
heads when Julia and Mrs. Moore appeared, though three
or four people right down below did look up and raise
their hands. Mrs. Moore nodded and smiled and just
slightly waved, so that it was perfectly natural for Julia
to begin pretending that she and Mrs. Moore were royalty
(the queen and the princess, or even better, the young
queen and the queen mother), gazing out benignly over
their subjects. In fact, with her coat put back over her
chair, her dusty pink velvet dress displayed (there were
other people behind them in the box, friends of Mrs.
Moore's, to whom she was talking), Aunt Alex's pearls

lying about her neck and her hands with their scrupulously clean nails crossed over the black silk evening purse, Julia felt extremely appropriate and attractive. Refusing to remember something Mrs. Moore had said in the taxi, she thought that she was as excited and happy, as content with herself, as it would ever be possible to be. That is, she thought, outside of the supreme happiness, of course, of going camping with Paul and his family in the Canadian Rockies. But that would never happen. And this *was* happening.

The members of the orchestra, already in their places on the stage, had been sending out for some time what Mrs. Moore called their "experimental pipings and scrannelings," which meant all those toots on horns and scrapings on stringed instruments they made as they tuned up. Now the mammoth chandeliers overhead dimmed, the audience hushed itself, the conductor strode forth and was tremendously applauded. And then something was played, very jumpy and discordant, which Julia thought horribly boring, and Oren Moore never came out once. She was enormously disappointed, not having thought to look at her program, but Mrs. Moore seemed not in the least perturbed and clapped heartily like everyone else when the piece was finished, though Julia could not understand for the life of her what there had been to be so enthusiastic about.

But now — now, the conductor held out his hand and here came Oren Moore at last, tall like his mother, erect, spare, with a thick mass of dark hair and the same deep-set eyes and high cheekbones. He stood receiving his own even more tremendous applause, then up came his head and his eyes met Mrs. Moore's. She did not move, nor lift her hand, but only smiled at him and the look that passed between them, Julia thought, as prickles rose along her arms, was enough. Of course now everybody turned and looked up, and Julia felt then that even she had a share in this unforgettable moment.

Oren Moore went to the grand piano and seated himself. The conductor lifted his baton, there was a second of tingling silence, and the music began — the Brahms Concerto in B Flat Major. Oren Moore sat at the piano with his head down, his hands folded, waiting for those musical phrases which would signal his own opening notes. And, as she had on the mountains above Berkeley, Julia remembered Mrs. Penhallow's words about seeing. "You must always *see* clearly —" and she began noticing how the conductor seemed to mold the music he was drawing from all those instruments, quieting it, smoothing it, putting his fingers to his lips, then calling it up again in full force with vigorous, powerful movements of the arms. The violinists and cellists, the men with their big double basses on the side, swept their bows, stopped, looked up quickly, then *swept* again. And every once in a while there came a majestic flood from all the strings together, welling and pouring out in a wave that was almost too much for Julia. She had heard records at home and in the music shop, but this experience of being directly in the path of an enormous tide of music was something she had never known before.

Now Oren Moore, in a hush, lifted his head, raised his hands — and began to play. Again the prickling rippled along Julia's arms. She felt Rhiannon Moore's hand cover hers, the fingers tightening, and Julia glanced round at her face, a pale oval of intense listening, her head up, her body straight, lifted with absorption and joy.

"I have been very unhappy, Julia," she'd said in the cab on the way to the theatre. "I am sorry I treated you as I did — it was unforgivable."

"No," said Julia. "I only wondered — I thought you were mad at me because of Ken getting in and going all over your house and playing the phonograph. I wrote to you —"

"And I got your note. But what Ken did was nothing — a mere thoughtless prank. At least I'm hoping that that was all it was, but I never blamed you for a moment, knowing the boy as I do. As for me, do you remember the night we became friends? Do you remember that I had a letter to mail, and that I said, 'Wish me luck'?"

"Oh, of course. I remember every single thing about that night. I'll never forget it."

Then, just as she had done now when her son began to play, Mrs. Moore had reached out and put her hand over Julia's.

"That letter was to my husband. I'd heard from his sister that he was sick, and because I could see no reason why we shouldn't take up our life together again and why he shouldn't come back to his own home where he belongs, I wrote and asked if I might go and see him and nurse him back to health if I could. As it turned out, I did go — and I did stay as long as he needed me. But in the end, when he was well again, he refused to come."

Julia waited for Mrs. Moore to go on; she seemed to be trying to decide how to explain.

"You see, Julia," she said finally, "he left many years ago and you can have no idea, being as young as you are, how people change. We are always deeply ourselves, but when two who have lived together with the same interests and friends are no longer together, they grow apart in many ways. They reach out in different directions, find different interests, so that after a while they have very little left in common. Now my husband has his own friends, his own life, his own little schedules and routines, and at his age he just doesn't want to change them. He's quite happy as he is. And nothing I could say made any difference. He was kind and regretful, but he would not come back —"

"But why did he *go?*" How could any husband have left a woman as beautiful and gifted as Rhiannon Moore, Julia wondered.

"Because I didn't consider him all those years ago when I was trying to become a concert pianist. And so finally he decided that if my music and my friends of that world, who were always filling our house and consuming my time when I wasn't practicing, were the most important part of my life, then he would go and leave me to them. Which he did."

"And did you love him, Mrs. Moore?"

"Very much — very, very much, I discovered after he'd left and refused to come back. But I'd gone on thinking, you see, that I could just live my own life without being too much concerned about whether he was happy or not. Or at least I didn't even realize, I saw later, that I wasn't being concerned. I hope you are never so blind, Julia, as to become that lost in your work. *Never so blind!*"

All at once it came into Julia's head what Greg had said to her on the ferry. She spoke without a moment's reflection.

"If your husband would come back, Mrs. Moore, then you wouldn't have to leave your house that your sister says is too big for you."

Mrs. Moore's hand slid away from Julia's.

"Well, I have no intention of leaving it anyway," she said. "But what made you think of that?"

"Greg. He said that the only reason I don't want my mother to marry Uncle Phil is so I won't have to give up my room, and not because of my father at all."

Mrs. Moore was quiet for a little, and then, "And *is* your mother going to marry Uncle Phil?"

"No, she's not. She said, 'Well, then, that's that,' when they quarreled in the basement at the music store."

"And you were glad, weren't you, Julia? But I happen to have met Uncle Phil by chance as he was coming out of your driveway one evening and we had quite a talk. I think you're wrong, Julia. I think you're wrong. Have you ever thought about your mother when you and Greg go your own ways? Have you ever thought about her as someone separate from yourself? Or is she simply an attachment, living for your own private use and benefit?"

To this, Julia had no answer.

The last direction Aunt Alex had given Julia before she left was to be sure to ask Mrs. Moore to come in for coffee when they got back from the concert. And when Uncle Hugh, having taken Julia down to the cab at the bottom of the walk, had introduced himself to Mrs. Moore and said what an extraordinary treat this was for her, he dutifully pressed the invitation. But he seemed embarrassed about not having got tickets and fumbled a bit at this point. After all, thought Julia, he couldn't very well tell Mrs. Moore he'd forgotten her *son*.

"You are so kind — very kind," Rhiannon Moore had said, looking up at Uncle Hugh out of her furs. "We shall see. It all depends upon Oren, of course — I believe something has been planned. But I do thank you."

And, no, she wouldn't come in, she said, when the cab drew up at the house again after the concert. In a heavy aroma of perfume and the impatient press of opera coats, jewel green, black, gold, scarlet, and the dark suits that accompanied them, Julia had gone backstage with her just as Mrs. Moore had promised. And Oren Moore, in the midst of all those silk and velvet coats and dark suits, had leaned down to Julia and told her how happy he was to meet his mother's friend and that he knew about her from his mother's letters. (About *me?* exclaimed Julia to herself in astonishment.) Had she enjoyed the concert? he wanted to know. Had she enjoyed sitting up in the box where she could look out over everyone? Had she ever sat in a box before?

"No," said Julia. "Never before. And it was — it was just —" But she couldn't think then how to put it all into words.

"I understand," he said, smiling. "You don't have to tell me. I'm so pleased."

Above her head, Rhiannon Moore and her son now began speaking in low voices while everybody else tried to edge her out of the way, but Julia stubbornly held her ground. Really, they seemed entirely unaware of her existence, never bothering to look down. Then, even as Mrs. Moore was saying, "All right, Oren, I'll be back soon — it won't take long, about half an hour. I couldn't let her go home in the cab alone, and I never thought to ask her uncle to come —" a high, piercing, female voice broke out: "Oren — Oren, my dear — it was *sim*ply *mar*velous — never have I —"

And Julia and Mrs. Moore got away.

"Don't gush, Julia. Don't ever be a gushing woman. However, at this point, it doesn't seem you'll grow up that kind."

Now it was all over; Julia was in the living room facing Aunt Alex.

"But where is Mrs. Moore?" she demanded in amazement, holding out her hands, palms up, as if she couldn't conceive of Rhiannon Moore rejecting her invitation.

Oh, golly! Hulda had everything ready — the silver teapot and coffee urn on the cart drawn up to one side of the fireplace, with cups and saucers and plates and little sandwiches and slices of fruitcake. The fire was going and firelight flickered on the silver, all so warm and cozy, especially with the foghorn beginning to send up its lonely bray somewhere out there among the cold, wet rocks.

"Aunt Alex, I'm sorry. She wouldn't come. She said she must get right back because they're having a party before Oren leaves for Los Angeles. She said he would be expecting her."

"Oren, Julia? *Mr. Moore!* I hope you didn't call him Oren to his face —"

"Oh, no — I didn't call him anything," said Julia, going over to the fire and taking off her coat. She had an eye on the fruitcake. "I couldn't even *say* anything. Much."

"Well, that's a blessing. And was it tremendous?"

"Yes," said Julia. Uncle Hugh held out the plate, Julia took a slice, and half of it disappeared in one bite. "Yes!" she said, chewing. "Everybody clapped like mad and stamped and yelled, 'Bravo! Bravo!' when he'd finished the last piece. And I wanted to yell, too, but I didn't have the nerve. And they kept calling him back and *calling* him back, and finally he played an encore, and then another, and that was the last."

"What did he play — what was the encore?"

But Julia couldn't remember. Then, "Oh, I know. Mrs. Moore — and she was just about crying, but she says she always does when the audience gets so worked up — Mrs. Moore said the first one was a Chopin nocturne —"

"The one," said Aunt Alex, leaning forward on the couch, "the one that has that delicate fall of minor notes — you know," and she sang them. "It's my favorite."

"Yes," said Julia. "That's exactly the one. And then he played something fiery and exciting for the last encore, and everybody stood up and cried 'Bravo!' all over again, but he wouldn't come out. There's the program over there with your purse."

"And tell me about Mrs. Moore," went on Aunt Alex. "What is she like — what was she wearing?"

"Well, she *wasn't* wearing any of her jewelry. She says she can't find her box that she keeps it in, and she wanted specially to wear something her friend, Mr. Yeats, gave her because Oren always liked it so."

"Mr. Yeats!" repeated Aunt Alex. "*What* Mr. Yeats? You don't mean —"

"Yes, William Butler Yeats, the poet. She knew him when she was young in Ireland, and he gave her a copy of his first book of poems and he wrote in it, 'For Rhiannon — wind and sea and sky all in one — Yours, W. B. Yeats.' She said that once when they were out walking, they stopped at an antique shop because she saw a heavy gold chain with a strange carved stone on it. It was in the window and because she admired it so, he got it for her. She said she doesn't care about losing anything else she has — only that."

Chapter Seventeen

When Julia woke the next morning, the house on its hill was like a boat floating on an ocean of fog. Muffled and still was the whole street, wound about with gray. The crowns of the trees lower down were drowned. Through the mist called, hollow and deep and mournful, the voice of the foghorn warning ships moving out to sea and those coming in through the Gate. She lay there curled up and warm in her bed thinking of how it would be telling Addie and Daddy Chandler and Mr. and Mrs. de Rizzio all about last night. And of course Leslie. She had promised to send Daddy a card and if she went with Uncle Hugh to the museum today, she could get one, though of course only to tell him a little so as to save most for when she got home and could make it a good, rich story.

But at breakfast — a leisurely breakfast, because this was Saturday morning — the telephone rang, and it was Mrs. Redfern calling to tell Julia that Daddy Chandler had died in the night, very peacefully in his sleep. Just when it was, Mrs. de Rizzio had said she didn't know.

Julia stood there with the receiver in her hand and could not speak.

"Julia?" said her mother. "You mustn't grieve, now. I know you loved him, but you have to remember he was in his eighties. He'd had a good life. A lot of people go before that. And he was happy and always so vigorous — chopping wood and having those wrestling matches with you and writing his book. And then going up —"

"But it's —" cried Julia in a stifled voice.

"What, dear?" No answer. "Julia, Daddy Chandler wouldn't want you to be mournful for him."

"But I wish I could come home."

Silence, while her mother thought.

"I have an errand in the city," she said, "on Monday, for the music store. You could come back with me then."

Late Monday afternoon Julia and Mrs. Redfern were sitting outside at the rounded stern of the ferry watching the churn of foam being shaken out in its wake. Its passage made a curving sweep across the bay from where it had left the San Francisco slip, but above that broad white path the fog was drifting in ever more thickly so that now the distant outlines of San Francisco were blotted out. The slap of the waves and the hushing sound they made along the side of the boat were muffled. Children on the far side of the deck were tossing bread to the gulls as they had on the voyage over, and their voices, calling now to the almost invisible birds and now to one another, had a lost and lonely sound as though they belonged not to real children but to the ghosts of children.

"Aunt Alex says you've hardly eaten, and that a good deal of the time you stayed in the bedroom with the door shut."

"Yes."

Mrs. Redfern was sitting a little sideways with her arm around Julia and Julia leaned against her, watching beyond the stern how the foam rippled and danced away behind. She had gone over in her mind, in the time since her mother phoned, all the tricks she'd played on Daddy, how when they'd gone for one of their walks in the hills, she'd climbed that big rock Kenny climbed, and when she got to the top, and Daddy was watching her, she'd pretended to slip and had disappeared down the other side with a sort of terrified, shocked cry — and then silence. Oh, she'd gotten that cry just right! And then she'd crouched there out of sight waiting to see what Daddy would do. But when he came around, his face was as white as it could possibly be, a dead white, and he came slowly as if he couldn't endure to see what he was sure he was going to. And she *wasn't* there on the ground in a heap the way he'd expected and so he looked up, and there she was grinning down at him, and she'd burst into shouts of laughter and yelled, "Fooled you, Daddy Chandler, fooled you!" But he hadn't laughed, and he said, "That wasn't a good joke, Julia — not a good joke at all." And she'd been so ashamed. How can you do things like that to people you care about? Another of her jokes was the time she'd asked him to come into the apartment and sit at the table while she went into the little coat closet, closed the door behind her, then very quietly got up on a box, climbed outside through the window and up the plumbing pipe to her mother's bedroom window (opened ahead of time) and came down the stairs, appearing as if by magic in the living room. He'd gasped, pretended to be shocked, overcome with astonishment, and then chuckled and chuckled and said wait till he told Zoë and Frank about that one. But as if he hadn't known by the racket her feet made on the wall outside what she was up to! And then they'd argued about religion, because Daddy firmly believed that the day would come when there would be no more death — not in heaven, but right here on earth — and Julia did not see how that could work. The world would get too full of everything, plants and animals and people, she said, but Daddy Chandler said the Lord would provide for that. And so the argument went on and on, with Julia becoming more and more vehement, until finally Daddy, looking exhausted, shook his head and got up and left. That was the only time she had ever felt he was really annoyed with her, as if her stubbornness and argumentativeness were too much for him and he wanted only to get away, back upstairs to his own peace and quiet. How many times Mrs. de Rizzio had told her she was apt to forget that Daddy was an old man — that she mustn't *go* at him so. But she hadn't, she hadn't! Only when *he* wanted to do things. But there was that time — that time when she'd wanted to hike up to Grizzly Peak, and she'd gone upstairs to ask Daddy to go, and Mrs. de Rizzio had said —

"Julia," began her mother. Julia waited. "Are you listening to me?"

"Yes —"

"Well, I want to tell you something. You're going to lose quite a few people you care about throughout your life. By death, and just because of the natural course of events — people change, or they move away. Now, considering Daddy's age, it seems to me that you're either indulging in self-pity or feeling guilty about something. I know you're troubled about him in some way, otherwise you wouldn't refuse to eat or speak. Can't you tell me?"

Julia turned and pressed her forehead into her mother's shoulder and then looked up and met that calm, candid, questioning gaze. She turned her own eyes away.

"It's Mrs. de Rizzio," she got out. The words were just above a whisper.

"What about Mrs. de Rizzio?"

"She always said that I was to — to remember that Daddy was an old man —"

"Well, you did, didn't you? All those little jokes you and he had — they weren't harmful. He loved them."

"Yes, I know. But she said once — she told me specially once when we were going up in the hills — that Daddy would never listen to her, as if she was lecturing him and making him feel old, but that he might listen to me. And she said if Daddy wanted to go for a hike I was to say we'd go another day, and then somehow not go. But I forgot, or at least I just didn't think, and we went. And then there was that day Daddy had to stop at the Carlsons' and rest, and Dr. Carlson drove us home because Daddy didn't feel like walking down, and he'd never — he'd *never* felt that way before. And then the woodshed joke. If I hadn't locked him in, he'd never have chopped all that wood. He chopped an awful lot, enough to last for weeks, all in one afternoon. And Mrs. de Rizzio told me she didn't want Daddy wrestling any more because it made him breathe so fast, but once or twice when she wasn't home, we — we did. He'd say, 'Come on, Julia — let's have a match —' "

Julia turned away, one foot curled under her, an arm up on the railing with her face buried against it to hide the fact from strolling passengers that she was crying. She cried long and bitterly and Mrs. Redfern said nothing at all, but just sat there waiting with her hand on Julia's leg. And when Julia had got over the worst of her grief, her mother gave her a handkerchief and Julia wiped her eyes and sat there sniffing and looking out across the bay toward Oakland. They were almost in. She could see the Berkeley hills and the big cement C, painted yellow, up on the hillside in back of the Greek Theatre, and the slim white campanile piercing up out of the dark green mass of the campus. The fog was still moving in. Soon Berkeley and Oakland, too, would be covered.

"I don't know, Julia," said her mother after a little. "Who could possibly say whether or not Daddy died before he had to? Or whether it was your fault. He was in his late eighties, and he did just what he wanted to do, except for being locked in the woodshed. He walked in the hills because he wanted to go, and he wrestled with you because he wanted to wrestle. You could have refused. But you cannot go on blaming yourself for the things a man Daddy's age chose to do. I think you should have listened to Mrs. de Rizzio — I think you should have remembered what she said. I can't soften that. You'll have to live with it. But I do honestly believe that Daddy Chandler lived just about as long as he would have if you'd never known him. And he was a happy and occupied person. He was never sick. He was just old."

That night Julia sat at her desk.

"*Strangeness:* I've just come back from Daddy Chandler's attic. Mrs. de Rizzio is going through his things and has given me the manuscript of his book all rolled around and tied with a string. She says nobody can read his writing and so I might as well have his book as long as I'm determined to send it off to a publisher. Mother says she doesn't see how I'm ever going to be able to read it, and I don't know if I can. I don't know what I'm going to do about a typewriter because Greg's always using his. When I came down from the attic into the hall Gretchy was there washing herself, and she followed me upstairs and hopped on my bed while I undid Daddy's book so I could start working on it. Gretchy had started licking herself again, and then maybe because she stopped, I turned around and there she was staring at something in the dark in Mother's room. I've seen her do this before, just for a second or two, then she goes on licking or purring or dozing or whatever it was she was doing. But this time she stared and stared, and sometimes her head or her eyes would move as if she was following whatever was moving in there. I twisted around to look, but there was nothing, and yet when I turned back to Gretchy, she was still watching. Not just looking off into space, but *watching*. And even when I said, 'Gretchy!' she never moved or stopped, so then I was scared because I thought it might be Daddy Chandler she could see, and I couldn't. But I thought, why should I be scared of seeing somebody I love, even though he's dead? And so I said in the direction of the darkness in Mother's room, 'Daddy, I have your book and I'll keep my promise.' Then I wanted to say more, about how I thought maybe I was to blame because he died and how sad I felt. But I was too frightened to, and was going to run downstairs because everything seemed so still, and then Gretchy started washing herself again. Could it have been Daddy in there? But if it was, why not in here with Gretchy and me, and why couldn't I see him the way Paul's father saw his brother's wife? Now Mother has just come up and says she doesn't think it was Daddy, and that cats often stare at nothing like that. But how do we know it's at nothing? And why did Gretchy's eyes move, and her head? What I want to know is, why was I scared of Daddy being there when I want him back again? I hope he knows how I feel and that I'm trying to read his book, but that maybe if his writing is too bad I can't keep my promise. What if he is depending on me?"

Chapter Eighteen

The next week was a quiet one, that is, until almost the end. Greg said that maybe by the time Julia had struggled her way through Daddy's manuscript — if ever she could, and he, personally, having taken a look at the pages, doubted it — he might have finished his Egyptian book and she could use the typewriter. She had never imagined, when the idea first came to her of working on Daddy Chandler's book, that she would be completely unable to read what he had written. She had thought, simply, that if she tried hard enough, as Mrs. de Rizzio never had, she would somehow be able to make out that curious, angular script. But she could not. It was as if she were trying to translate some foreign language. Here and there, words, sometimes bits of sentences, came through, but:

245

"It's too much for a child, Julia," her mother said when she sat down in front of that stack of pages and flipped through them. "It's too *much* — it would be too much for me, so then how can you expect to do it? I mean, how will you be able to stick with it? You mustn't be ashamed of giving up."

"But I promised him!" insisted Julia, her cheeks flaming and even her eyes hot with frustrated effort. "I promised him, that day I got Mrs. Penhallow's letter about going up to see her, and I took it in to show Daddy and he said I was really going to be a writer but he knew he'd never see his book published. And I said I'd learn to type and that I would type out his whole manuscript and send it off for him if he died before *he* could. And what was the use of his working all that time if it was to be all for nothing!"

Even as she said these words the smell of heat-baked rafters was in her memory, the smell of Daddy's fresh linen, the cologne he used and the white peppermints he had always kept in a paper bag in his pocket. She could see the fresh pink of his cheeks and how his hair had always stood up in fluffs around his head when he'd been working hard, the papery thinness of his lids with their sparse white lashes, and the expression of his pale blue eyes, the teasing and merriment and affection in them whenever he looked at her. There had been a fly droning around the attic and she could hear, even now, at the back of her mind, the way it had bumped and zizzed and buzzed through the sunlit afternoon in and out of the slants of light sloping in through the western windows, and how a rafter would crack here and then after a while give a loud pop over there. Daddy's attic. "Mrs. de Rizzio says he's been writing on those big sheets of paper for months and months, maybe years, and all for nothing — all for nothing —"

Mrs. Redfern was sitting at Julia's desk, the lamp shining up on her face, and she was studying Julia where she had thrown herself flat on her back on the bed.

"I know somebody else who wrote and wrote — all for nothing, you might say —"

"My father."

"Yes. But I have a feeling it wasn't all for nothing. When your father was lost in his work, the way Daddy Chandler was lost in his, he wouldn't have exchanged his life for any other. Those were the happy times, even though it's a battle to write what one truly sees and feels. It was the work itself that counted above everything else, and not what would happen to it. And that's the way it was with Daddy. He knew he'd die before he could see his book sent off. But he had to keep going because he was reliving the past, calling it up all around him right there in his attic, and it was the great pleasure of his days to wake every morning and know that he could go on struggling to shape the past on paper as near his heart's desire as he possibly could. That's what meant most to him — the doing of it."

Maybe, thought Julia, *may*be. But she would not give up work on his book — not just yet. And she went on tugging away at his writing, penciling in above his own whatever words she could make out, and always being teased on — teased on — by small successes.

And sometimes she would work on "The Harpet," because now, of all times, it had chosen in its own perverse way to begin to come clear, and to appear to her not any longer as a short story but as a whole book with chapters: her first real book. Perhaps it was becoming clear because now she understood more about the harpet itself, and continued to understand more: how it was not simply some vague sort of being, but a bird. Not a beautiful bird so much as an unusual one, such a bird as the boy in the story had never seen or heard of, whose call was five clear, falling tones like no other, and that always compelled the boy to listen and wish with his whole being that he might hear it again — and again. After a while he began to notice that the bird came only at certain times, when he was unhappy because of certain mysterious occurrences in his family that he could not understand. And he wondered if the bird was trying to call attention to itself by its call, and then trying to tell him something by the way it stayed around the garden, and its odd way of looking at him and hopping always just beyond his reach. What *was* it trying to tell him? In his wonderment and in his looking and listening, he began to hear and notice things he did not usually hear and notice. And it was all these things, these little hidden, secret sights and sounds, that gradually brought the boy to understand at last what was wrong between himself and his brother and mother and father.

248

It was not an easy story to write, but very exciting, and when Julia could not keep herself from telling Mrs. Redfern one evening the idea of it, and reading just the beginning to her (which she had started all over again when she realized her story was to be a book), her mother looked at her across the dining table, where they had been sitting talking after dinner, and shook her head.

"An extraordinary idea, Julia. And there're to be chapters! How am I to wait until it's finished! I wonder if *St. Nicholas* takes serials."

Sometimes, when there came a certain moment in the middle of the afternoon or toward the end of it when she had no more energy to write, she would go off to Addie's to see if things were any different. Something was wrong over there. She had gone three times and the first time, Gram, grim-faced, had said that Addie had housework to do. The second time Addie herself had answered the door and said that no, she didn't want to play. And the third time Mr. Kellerman had come round the side of the house and fixed her with his haunted, staring eyes while her hand hovered over the doorbell and then drew back. "That'll do," he'd said, because she'd been calling Addie, and Julia darted off the porch and away home.

Now, today, around five o'clock of a Saturday afternoon with only one more week of summer vacation ahead, she sat at her desk where she had been writing out, in the *Book of Strangenesses,* all about why she felt something must have happened at Addie's house. Idly she watched Greg down in the back garden bouncing the bamboo rake

along the freshly mown lawn as if he were an idiot boy.
But he was thinking, Julia knew, and hadn't the least idea
(and wouldn't have cared if he had) how idiotic he looked
bouncing that bamboo rake. He did all sorts of peculiar
things when he was thinking, like twisting one corner of
his hair into a peak or crackling the pages of books, which
made Mrs. Redfern desperate, or whistling little soft, off-
key, monotonous tunes. Now all at once he came to, finished raking up the grass, arranged it around the base of
the rose bushes, and went off to the front of the house
with the pruning shears.

At that moment Mrs. Moore, who had arrived home
about an hour before from San Francisco where she'd been
visiting friends ever since her son left, came out of the
back door of her house in her dressing gown. She walked
"in an awfully shrunken up sort of way," Julia told her
mother afterwards, over to the fence with her hands
clasped together, held up to her mouth, and an expression
on her face as if she'd been hit in the pit of the stomach.
She looked all around, apparently expecting Greg still to
be there somewhere. Then she looked up at Julia's windows and at once Julia got up and went out onto the balcony.

"Mrs. Moore, what's the matter? What's happened?"

"Julia — I've done the most terrible thing. An unforgivable thing —" And Rhiannon Moore put her face in
her hands and just stood there. And she stayed like that
as if she was never going to look up or ever move from
that spot again.

Julia turned and went back in, tore down the stairs, out into the garden, across the grass and opened the gate. And then Mrs. Moore took her hands away and reached out and got hold of Julia's arm and drew her close.

"I've found my jewelry," she said almost in a whisper. "I've found it — just — exactly — where I put it when I left to take care of my husband that time he was ill. Oh, child, run over quick to the Kellermans'. Tell them! Tell them!"

"But, Mrs. Moore," exclaimed Julia, completely baffled, "what have the Kellermans —"

"I should never have said a word to Mrs. Kellerman," went on Mrs. Moore, looking away as if speaking to herself. "Even while I was telling her about my jewel box missing, I *knew* I shouldn't. But I was sick about losing the chain with the stone that Mr. Yeats gave me. If it hadn't been for that — just for that — I don't believe I'd ever have said a word. And now Kenny's gone off, Mrs. Kellerman told me on the phone when I called her from San Francisco to see if she'd found out anything yet. And it was because of his father. Run, Julia — run quick. Tell them! They don't seem to have a phone in the house —"

And so Julia, trying confusedly to put it all together, ran as fast as she could, calling out to Greg as she passed the front lawn, where he was whacking away at bushes with the pruning shears, that Mrs. Moore had "found all her stuff." And when she got to the Kellermans' and nobody answered the bell, she ran around to the back and heard Mr. Kellerman carrying on in the kitchen.

Terrified as she was at the sound of his voice, but filled
with the fire of her mission and determined as well to
know what was happening, she went in. And there stood
little old Grammy at the end of the table near the stove,
Mr. Kellerman on the side near the windows with his head
weaving back and forth like an enraged bull's, and Mrs.
Kellerman on the side near the front hall door with her
coat still on as if she'd just got home from work. Mr. Kellerman's face was all drawn up and his arms were lifted as
if he was about to batter something down.

"— sick of hearing about that kid," he was yelling. "Always the kid — everything the kid. If he's a thief, let
him go — let him be — what d'you care? When I was
fourteen I was taking care of myself. I should think you'd
be glad to see the last of him — never come to no good,
that kid wouldn't. Always sleek and sly and lyin' and
slippin' in and outa places, the little runt. Never would
meet a person head on, or look him in the eye —"

"Because he never dared," shouted Mrs. Kellerman, her
voice shaking, but going on just the same. "Never dared,
because he couldn't stand up to you — you never let him
talk, never let him explain or say anything. He could have
been right, but *you'd* never listen. And who are you to talk
about Kenny coming to no good! Who are *you* — never
done a day's work in years, drinking when you couldn't
face yourself any more and then coming downstairs and
bellering at Kenny and Addie and Gram and me — like
now. *Look* at you — *look at you* — standing there, a bunch
of clothes full of nothing. *Nothing,* d'you hear me? Who

are you to say somebody else'll never come to no good —!"

At that instant Mr. Kellerman's arms swooped down, he grasped the table's edge and it began rising, slow motion. And in slow motion, all the plates and bowls of food, which Gram had apparently just put on, and all the knives and forks and spoons and glasses, began sliding down the cloth, with the cloth wrinkling and the food spilling out and then falling, while Gram and Mrs. Kellerman, with their hands out, darted forward and made little futile, scrabbling motions. Then there was a crash as everything went on the floor and the table toppled and plunged over on top of the food and broken china and glass, while Gram and Mrs. Kellerman screamed and Mr. Kellerman stood there in front of the windows with his arms lifted again and a look on his face of fierce, blazing triumph.

For just an instant, right after the table went over and Gram and Mrs. Kellerman stopped screaming and stood staring down at the wreckage as if they couldn't believe what had happened, there was a taut, ringing silence. And in that silence Julia spoke.

"But he's not a thief," she said. "Kenny's not. Mrs. Moore's found her things, right where she put them. Kenny didn't take them. She said to tell you."

Her eyes went flicking around, quick, from one face to another and then back to Mr. Kellerman's, and she would never forget the look that came over it. He went gray, a sick greenish gray, and his eyes in their hollow caverns seemed to change until they were like two black staring stones.

"She's lyin'," came from his lips in a broken burst of sound. "She's lyin', that woman is, for the kid's sake, to save his hide —"

"No," cried Julia, and she came further into the room, her heart floundering so madly in her chest it seemed as if it was trying to get out. "She's not — I know she's not. I know by the way she came out of the house and the way she told me. She's *found* them —"

At this, Mr. Kellerman suddenly lunged forward, knocking over his chair and then blundering around it, kicking one of the legs and stumbling. He shoved Grammy to one side and went out the back into the scullery and kept on going through the laundry porch and they heard the screen door slam.

"Let me go to her," said Mrs. Kellerman. "I must talk to her — to Mrs. Moore."

And Gram came along too, her little eyes kindling with wrath, her apron flapping in the wind, striding along in her high, laced-up black shoes with the flat heels, and her long skirts whipping around her legs. Mrs. Kellerman hurried beside her, sobbing under her breath, "Kenny — Kenny —" and Julia ran just in front of Mrs. Kellerman, glancing back every now and then to see how it was with them.

When they got to Rhiannon Moore's, she was standing on the front porch where she'd been watching for them and she had her arms gripped around herself as if she were trying to keep herself together.

"Mrs. Kellerman," she said, and came down the steps, and hooked one hand under Gram's arm and one under Mrs. Kellerman's and took them inside and Mrs. Kellerman burst into tears. But Gram didn't. Her face was just as small and tight and clamped down as it always was and she strode into the house and sat down on a chair and waited to be explained to. Mrs. Moore drew Mrs. Kellerman down onto the couch with an arm around her, and Julia stood there in the middle of the floor looking at everyone, and then around at Greg and her mother, who had just come in the back door and through the kitchen and dining room. Mrs. Redfern went over to the couch and sat down on the other side of Mrs. Kellerman, and Greg drew up a chair and sat near them.

"I will do anything I can," Mrs. Moore was saying. "Anything — anything at all — to get Kenny back. Believe me, Mrs. Kellerman, I don't care what it costs, or what it involves —"

"But where *is* he?" burst out Mrs. Kellerman when she could speak. "That's what I want to know. *Where is he?* He's been gone for almost a week now and never a word from him. Not a word — not a word — and I didn't dare tell the police he was gone —"

"He's all right," said Greg, and he reached out and touched her knee, and everybody lifted their heads with their mouths fallen open. "He's all right. I've been wanting to tell you. I've been wanting to tell all of you, but I couldn't. I promised Ken on my word of honor I wouldn't until he got up to the ranch because he was afraid you'd get the police after him and stop him and bring him back. But I can tell now because you know he didn't take anything. He was afraid — I've never seen anyone so afraid."

"Greg," said his mother, "*Greg* — how could you do a thing like that!" She seemed, Julia thought, to be shriveling inside herself.

"But I promised. I promised him, and I wasn't going to go back on that. He came to me for help, and you should have seen him. His father had knocked him around and his face was bruised, and he said his arm hurt and that he was never going back to that house again — never in his life — and that he hadn't taken Mrs. Moore's stuff but nobody would believe him. I don't know why I believed him, but I just did. He was like that rabbit up in the hills that was caught by the legs and then screamed when we all closed in on it. And I thought he should have a chance, so I let him have the money I had in my room, forty dollars what with my birthday money from Uncle Hugh and Aunt Alex and the fifteen dollars I'd saved up from gardening that I kept meaning to put in savings but I never had. I believed Ken when he said he'd pay me back as soon as he could after he got up to his uncle's ranch and could work and get something —"

"All that way," breathed Mrs. Kellerman.

"Yes, all that way," said Greg. "He was going to hitchhike, and he needed money for food, or he said maybe he'd get a train ticket for part of the trip. And I thought — everybody always blamed Ken for everything because they were used to doing it. And I thought about him going after

256

that rabbit, and nobody wanting him to have it, and then what Dr. Carlson said afterwards about what difference would it make if he *had* caught it and put it in a cage and fed it. There are millions of rabbits in cages and hutches and nobody ever thinks anything about it. But because Ken wanted it, and yelled out it was his, we didn't like that and kept him away from it when maybe it would have been a good thing for him to have a pet to take care of. Of course it was wild and might have died — so I don't know. Anyway, then he left us and went on down home, feeling frustrated and mean and all in the wrong again, the way he always feels. And I thought about Paul, how quiet he always was with Ken, and that Paul'd be good for him because he never raised his voice or got really mad at him. Just explained, and took Ken the way he took everybody else — not as if Ken was some kind of ornery little weasel that you always had to kick out of the way or hit or yell at no matter what he did. Paul was good with him, and so was Paul's father. And it just seemed to me you can get *used* to treating some people a certain way and they have to change from that kind of life to get any different. I don't know — but that's what I thought."

Mrs. Kellerman leaned forward.

"You could have told *me*, Greg," she said.

"No, I couldn't. I didn't know what you'd do. You made one mistake when you went home knowing Mrs. Moore's jewelry had disappeared after Ken was in this house. And you went at him about it because you just took it for granted he'd taken it and that it had something to do with those kids he went around with. And you weren't careful and Mr. Kellerman heard and that's why he went for Ken. I couldn't trust you. So I just kept quiet about the whole thing. And he's all right, because I had a letter from him this morning and he's almost there. He's going to have your sister phone me the minute he arrives — the first night he arrives, so we'll be sure to be at home. I don't know — he might even phone tonight because his letter was mailed two days ago."

Mrs. Kellerman got up.

"I'm going to go," she said. "I'm going to go up to Norm's in Canada — that's what I'll do, right away. I'm going to pack up and take Addie."

"If you do, then I shall buy the tickets," said Rhiannon Moore. "You must please let me do that, Mrs. Kellerman. I'll get round trip — whatever you want."

"No, I wouldn't want round trip, Mrs. Moore. There'd be no need for that. We wouldn't be coming back."

Chapter Nineteen

Who would ever have imagined that, not Julia, but Addie
— of all people, *Addie* — would be the one to leave their
street first! Julia couldn't get over it. And not just leave
their street, and not just leave Berkeley, and not just leave
California, but leave the *country* to go clear up and live
in Canada near Paul and see the high mountains with the
glaciers on them. To think of that!

"Everything is strange," she wrote in her *Book of
Strangenesses, "everything."* Because if she had never had
a dream, she would never have written "The Mask," and
if she hadn't written "The Mask," she would never have
gone out to mail it, and if she hadn't gone out to mail it at
the same time Mrs. Moore went to mail her letter and Mr.

Kellerman went out to get some air, she and Mrs. Moore might not have become friends. And if they hadn't become friends, then Mrs. Moore wouldn't have given Julia the key to her house so that Julia could go in and water the plants, and if Julia hadn't had the key to be forgetful about and leave in the lock of the door, Ken would never have got in and played his trick. And if he hadn't got in, he wouldn't have been blamed for stealing Mrs. Moore's jewels, and his father would never have beaten him the way he did, and he wouldn't have run away to Canada, and Mrs. Kellerman would never have decided to go too.

"It almost looks as if your dream," said Greg, "will have caused Ken and Addie and Mrs. Kellerman all to go to Canada. *Maybe,*" he added, "because you couldn't know what other things might have happened if these hadn't."

Julia caught her breath in wonderment. You could hardly believe it — but there it was.

"It's the same as chess," said Greg. "Every single move affects what all the other pieces can do. Every move determines the end in a way no ordinary player can see. But a chess master can. I wonder if there are life masters. I wouldn't want to be a life master — I couldn't stand it. I should think it would be impossible to do anything. You wouldn't have the courage."

After this conversation, Julia had so much to put into the *Book of Strangenesses* she thought she would never finish, and her writing got worse and worse, and by the time she'd come to the end (but not really the end, because there semed to be no end — her thoughts kept going on and on), she was exhausted.

Kenny didn't phone the night of the day Mrs. Moore found her box of jewelry, but he did phone the next night and Julia ran fast over to the Kellermans' to get Mrs. Kellerman and Addie. And even though Uncle Norm was a wealthy man and even though Greg and Mrs. Redfern were talking to Ken and Ken was being told they knew he didn't take anything, the thought of all those hideously expensive minutes leaking away was an awesome thing to have in your mind. But there at last were Ken and Mrs. Kellerman joined up, and at first all Mrs. Kellerman could say was, "Oh, Ken — Ken — are you all right? Oh, it's so *good* to hear your voice! Are you perfectly all right?"

And he was, only sometimes it had been hard to get good hitches, he said — people going a long enough distance in his direction so that he didn't keep being dropped off and have to stand for another couple of hours or so, wondering if he was ever going to make it. Twice he'd slept out in fields because he didn't like picking up hitches in the dark, but mostly he'd got in with friendly people, some of them driving his way all night, till they had to turn off, and if there was a woman in the car she was usually the most interested and would ask all sorts of questions about his age and everything because he looked younger than he really was. Once he'd got in with two men he didn't like at all, and that was the worst time. It wasn't anything they'd actually said or done, but he was so frightened of them for some reason it made him feel sick, so when they stopped for gas and one went to the bathroom and the other got out to go into the station for a map, he'd slipped out the door on the road side and whipped across the street and in behind some buildings, then kept going on out into the country. And he'd never seen those men again.

At first he didn't seem to know what to say when he found that his mother and Addie were coming up to Canada too, but then he sounded pleased, Mrs. Kellerman said afterwards, and of course her sister was overjoyed. They were to stay at the ranch as long as they liked, she said, until Mrs. Kellerman found the right job and the right apartment or flat to rent. But, she said, there was no hurry and why couldn't her sister have a good, long vacation and take it easy and have fun for a while?

When Mrs. Kellerman finally hung up, she stood there staring at everybody as if she couldn't get it through her head that her life was about to undergo a complete change and that maybe everything was going to be better. This was hard to take in, possibly — as Greg said afterwards — because she was too used to being unhappy. And all the time she was standing there with a dazed look on her face, Addie was going wild, dashing around and around the Redferns' little living room yelling, "We're going — we're going — we're going — and Ken's all *right!*"

And then she and Mrs Kellerman went next door to tell Mrs. Moore that Ken had called and to make the decision as to just when they would be ready to leave so that Mrs. Moore could get the train tickets, because she had the time to do this and Mrs. Kellerman didn't, what with so much to finish up at work and at home just as soon as possible. She was like Addie: she couldn't wait to get away.

On the day of departure, Uncle Phil came good and early to drive Addie and her mother over to the station in Oakland. Mrs. Kellerman said she didn't care how early he came, just as long as there would be plenty of time in case of blowouts and other car trouble. So there, at seven in the morning, was Uncle Phil outside the Kellermans', putting Mrs. Kellerman's luggage in the car. And Mrs. Moore was there, of course, and all the Redferns. Julia, naturally, was going to drive over to be with Addie as long as possible and to have the excitement of seeing her off, and Mrs. Redfern was going too. She and Uncle Phil would drive right to work when they got back. There was no sign of Mr. Kellerman, but Gram was out there on the sidewalk with her big apron on as usual and her arms folded, watching everything go into the car with an everyday expression on her tight little face. Not one bit of difference. But when the suitcases and three boxes done up with cord were stowed away and it came time for Addie to get in, all at once she held out her arms and Addie flew to her and gave her a long hug and a fervent kiss on her white cheek.

"Now, girl, you be good — and tell Kenny — you tell Kenny —" but she never finished. And Julia was stunned to see that her small jetty eyes were brimming with tears, which she snatched away with the corner of her apron. Then Mrs. Kellerman went to her and took her hands, and Gram held on for a second, but just as Mrs. Kellerman bent over the little figure, Gram stepped back. She'd had enough of *that* with Addie!

"Good-bye," called Mrs. Moore as they were about to drive off, "good-bye, and good luck — oh, *good* luck!" She kissed her hands to them, and Greg stood there between her and Gram, a little taller than Mrs. Moore but not much, and towering over Gram, who never moved, never lifted an arm but just stood there with her hands clasped under her apron — three figures in the early sun slanting through the trees and across the quiet lawns and houses.

"*Well* — we'll never see *that* place again," said Mrs. Kellerman with satisfaction when they came to the corner, "nor ever see this street, and I've lived here for sixteen years and in this neighborhood all my life."

"And *now*," said Addie, "I don't have to worry and feel sad any more about you moving away, Julia. I don't have to think a thing about it," and she threw her arms up as if she was free as the air.

"And *were* you thinking and feeling sad and worrying?" exclaimed Julia. She'd never noticed any sign of it.

"Well, naturally," said Addie. "My best friend! And you moving up by Leslie, and you and Leslie seeing each other all the time, and her writing poetry. What d'you suppose? You'd have forgotten me."

"I would *not* have!" cried Julia. "I wouldn't! You'd always be my best friend."

Addie gave her a dry little look out of the corner of her eye. "No," she said, and looked down and smoothed her dress. "No, I wouldn't. But anyhow, now it doesn't matter — and you and Leslie can *be* best friends and that's OK with me."

"But do you mean we're going to stop, Addie?"

"No — we'll write. And it'll be fun sending you a birthday present from Canada."

Julia had completely forgotten, life being so full, that her birthday was, indeed, only two weeks away.

"And I won't be handing you my present, Julia," said Uncle Phil. "Somebody else will give it to you — I don't know who and I don't know when."

Now Addie was gone. The train had drawn out, Addie had sat at the window waving, her face joyous, and her mother leaned forward on the other side and waved too, smiling, and the smile would fade and then come back again as if she were thinking how maybe there was a chance now, though you couldn't depend upon it, that Ken would change. There was just a chance.

On the return to Berkeley, Julia was quiet. How had Addie known, she wondered, that she was going to move away when she had not once told Addie anything about all that had happened between Uncle Phil and her mother, and when she, Julia, hadn't even thought about moving? (But hadn't she, even though neither Greg nor her mother had spoken of it?) So then her mother must have told Mrs. Kellerman, and it was all settled. And Julia had just been pushing the knowledge away as if, now that Uncle Phil was coming around again, it might happen far off in the distance sometime, but who knew when?

Uncle Phil drew up in front of the music store and parked, and after Mrs. Redfern and Julia got out, Julia drew her back so that Uncle Phil went in alone. They were standing by the big white Victor dog at the corner of the window and Julia worked with her fingernail at the dust that had settled in behind its ear.

"Mother, are you and Uncle Phil going to get married?"

"Yes, Julia — we are."

"When?"

"I'm not quite sure. It all depends on the house being finished, but I should think in a month or so." Silence, while Julia kept working away at the dust. "Do we have your blessing?"

Julia did not look up. "I guess that doesn't come into it."

"Oh, yes it does. I must do what I think is right, but I can't be happy, really happy, until I have your blessing."

"Then," said Julia in a muffled voice because she could

scarcely get out the words, "then — you have it," and she turned and went off down the street toward home.

And when she came to the corner outside Mrs. Moore's she saw the postman walking away to the Parcels' house, and there was a magazine rolled up and lodged in the two hooks under the Redferns' mailbox next to the de Rizzios' on the side of their front porch. Julia went along the driveway and pulled the magazine out, and it was *St. Nicholas* and it was addressed to her. There, printed on the label stuck to the brown wrapper, were her name and address. So then this was what Uncle Phil had meant — his birthday gift to her would be given her by someone he didn't know and he had no idea when. With a feeling of serene fatefulness, Julia slipped off the wrapper and opened *St. Nicholas* near the back — and there, there, of course, as she knew it would be, was her story, "The Mask," by Julia Caroline Redfern of Berkeley, California. How long it was! How much type it had taken — almost a page and a half! And how beautiful it was! Julia lifted the magazine to her nose and smelled deeply of the rich, clean fragrance of glossy magazine paper and printer's ink. Idly, as she tried to take in her whole story at once, she reached inside the box and drew out one letter, all that was there — and it was for her, from Paul. And when Mrs. Moore came out on the veranda to get her own mail and looked over and saw Julia's face:

"Why, Julia, what is it?"

"Mrs. Moore," said Julia, "what did you call it when you and I came home that first night we met and we heard the birds in the sky? You said it was a certain kind of time, just a little space that meant something special —"

"A moment of being, I said."

"Yes," said Julia, "that's it. That's what this is, right now — a moment of being."

Chapter Twenty

Strangeness: I have just said good-bye to Mrs. Moore. I had to because she has an appointment and we'll be gone by the time she gets back — I mean for good. And I've said good-bye to the de Rizzios, but we'll have them all up after we move. And now I'm going to write down here all Mrs. Moore said before I forget because it's complicated.

"She's been thinking about my mask story and my father being a writer and such a complex man (that's what she called him after I got through telling her about him and some of the the things I remembered that I didn't tell Mother I remembered) and she said my dream's fascinating. I told her what I said to Greg on the boat, that my father being a writer had maybe handed on his mask to me. And I told her I didn't think what I was saying, but

just said it — and why *did* I when I didn't really understand? The thing is — I thought masks hide, yet when
you're writing something, you're telling about yourself,
not hiding. But Mrs. Moore said, not necessarily. Because
in writing you can reveal yourself *or* hide yourself, and
you might not know which you're doing. You could hide
and mean to, or hide and not mean to. Or you could reveal
and mean to, or reveal and not mean to. And also masks
can hide or reveal things about you. It would be the kind
of mask you chose, she said. And I said, but why did I
shut the door in my dream and then lean against it so
frightened, after the man gave me the mask? And she said
that maybe the mask was not only his desire to write but
his whole difficult complex self that he's handed on to
me — the things Grandmother didn't like in him, I guess,
and that I think she doesn't like in me. And Mrs. Moore
says I must make the difficult part work in my writing.
Always make it *work,* she said.

"And I said, if my dream *did* mean this about my father
and me — but there's no knowing — how could I dream
something I don't understand about masks and writing,
and the mask and my father? And Mrs. Moore said that
that was like my saying to Greg on the boat something I
didn't understand, and that if I do turn out to be a writer,
and a good one, I'll always be pulling things out of myself that I didn't know I knew and that I don't know I
understand.

"I wonder if this is the way it's going to be! If it is,
which would be exciting, but hard, too, Mrs. Moore says,

very, very hard, then I am surely going to be one. I wouldn't miss it for anything.

"These are the last words written in my room made of windows (I'll always remember Greg saying that), and I am sitting on the floor with my back against the light well and all the furniture is gone and everything is bare and hollow and echoing. Now I have got to get the cats because Greg is calling me and Uncle Phil is down there and we have to go."